LOCKDOWN

SCI-FI #2

Compiled & Edited by

Ben Thomas | D. Kershaw
Maggie Pawsey | S.N. Graves

Also available and coming soon
from Black Hare Press

DARK DRABBLES ANTHOLOGIES

WORLDS
ANGELS
MONSTERS
BEYOND
UNRAVEL

APOCALYPSE
LOVE
HATE
OCEANS
ANCIENTS

BHP WRITERS' GROUP SPECIAL EDITIONS

STORMING AREA 51
EERIE CHRISTMAS

BAD ROMANCE
TWENTY TWENTY

OTHER VOLUMES

DEEP SPACE
WHAT IF?
KEY TO THE
KINGDOM

DEEP SEA
BEYOND THE REALM

Twitter: @BlackHarePress
Facebook: BlackHarePress
Website: www.BlackHarePress.com

Cover design	Dawn Burdett	www.dmburdett.com
Formatting	Ben Thomas	www.blackharepress.com
Editing	D. Kershaw	www.blackharepress.com
	Maggie Pawsey	
	S.N. Graves	www.sngraves.com
Read Team	Alice Lam	www.alicelambooks.com
	David Green	davidgreenwritercom.wordpress.com
	Holley Cornetto	
	Jennifer Hatfield	jhatfieldauthor.wixsite.com/website
	Jodi Jensen	jodijensenwrites.wordpress.com
	Lyndsay Ellis-Holloway	authorlyndseyellisholloway.webador.co.uk
	Stacey Jaine McIntosh	www.staceyjainemcintosh.com

TABLE OF CONTENTS

A WHOLE NEW WORLD

By Amber M. Simpson

We wake from our sleep pods—stiff, sore, but ready. Immediately, we are ushered into the ship's conference room, briefed once again on our mission. Soon we will land on the new planet and the procedure once there is simple: kill or imprison all those in our way as we work to claim the new land as our own.

When the time comes, we all huddle at the portholes, straining to get a good look. And there it is, in the distance, just as beautiful as they said it would be. Earth, it is called, and soon will be ours.

TOMORROW

By D.M. Burdett

The storm passed through the bay, drenching everything in its path and filling the night with a cacophony of deafening drums.

Lightning shattered across the cloudless sky, and the wind whipped debris into swirling clouds around me as I stumbled down the embankment of the overpass. I steadied myself against the wall, the weight of Ella's body threatening to topple me into the swelling waters of the Yarra with every precarious step.

I ducked under the Wesgate Ridge sign, stepping into the gap under the overpass and out of the deluge, just as my legs finally gave out. I dropped to my knees, my hands skidding in the mud, almost not catching my weight, and Ella's body slid slowly, carelessly from my shoulders. My vision swam in the darkness while her dead eyes watched, unblinking.

The first wave of convulsions wracked my body, and I vomited bloody mucus into the wet dirt until dry heaves left me wheezing and breathless.

As the dizziness abated, I gulped cold gasps of damp air into my lungs.

Ella, in life, had been a tiny slip of a girl. Lithe and strong, the fiercest of soldiers, was tiny even so. But I was fatigued and malnourished, and not used to the unfiltered air outside of the city walls.

And she was all dead weight now.

When I felt able, I pulled her swathed body to the water's edge and mumbled a brief epitaph as I pushed it into the choppy water.

"Stand down, soldier," I whispered.

I watched for a moment as the bundle bobbed on the current before the Yarra's movements slowly pulled her out into the turbulent flow, and out to sea.

The river was no proper burial for a soldier of Fomalhaut, but there was little choice in these dark times. If the Sapiens found a burial pyre, they would know that we'd been here. Know that we were out here somewhere.

They would come for us, hunt us down.

I left the overpass then, dragging myself back up the bank to the road above, the rain pummelling me all the while.

As I stood at the junction, I looked back across the river. The storm drowned out the gunfire and the engines, but flashes of light spattered across the landscape on the far side. I watched as an explosion erupted somewhere near the old docks, lighting up the decimated remnants of the New Melbourne skyline.

They'd taken the city.

The domed metropolis was all but

gone. Only shattered obelisks of the thick wall still remained in testament to the life we'd built on Earth over the last two hundred years. Two hundred years since we'd come here to help the human survivors of their last war. To help them rebuild the fractured ruins of the planet they almost destroyed. We'd made a new home. For them and for us.

I turned and headed back to the old pumping station wearily, the rain beating me down as I staggered through the deserted streets.

I dropped into the basement of the ancient ruins just as Tara's scream echoed through the dark corridors the sound cutting through the thunder. *Fuck! She's gonna get us all killed.*

The sound followed me as I shuffled through the underground labyrinth of corridors, stooped low against the torn ceiling above, before shouldering open the rusting door to the room that we'd taken refuge in the night before. Neither Brad nor Tara looked up when I entered.

"The city's gone. They're still taking a lot of fire over by the docks, though." I sat down heavily on a concrete slab that butted out from the damaged wall and shrugged off my armour. "Whoever's over there is keeping the Sapiens busy."

Brad nodded, but I could see that he wasn't listening. He touched Tara's cheek tenderly and his thumb, blue and opaque, rubbed across her pale, white cheek. Not for the first time, I was reminded of the peeled, boiled egg of a chicken that the Sapiens seemed to eat so frequently. She gurgled another loud groan through clenched teeth, her eyes squeezed shut, and her jaw clenched as her fingers dug into his arm.

"How's she doing?" I asked, although I didn't care. This Sapien was holding us back, giving us problems we didn't need. If it weren't for her, we'd be on the M route by now. And we'd be a man up.

Brad and I were among the first Fomalhaut settlers to land on the planet after the humans almost nuked themselves out of existence in 2020. We came with love and empathy, our aim only to help, each of us chosen by our people for our fortitude, our respect, our science. When we left our planet, we knew it was a one-way ride; it would be a long time before the Sapiens would have the technology that would help us to get home.

We were met with suspicion but, once the Sapiens realised we were not a threat—we had come to build, not fight—they welcomed us with open arms. They embraced our technologies and our compassion and learned how to live together in harmony, as we once did on Fomalhaut.

But Hautians live longer than humans, and the friends we made in those early days grew old and died. We loved and cared for their children and grandchildren, but most of them are gone too. And now age is finally starting to take a hold on us.

Successive generations of Sapiens didn't understand the extent of what had happened in World War III, of just how devastated human life had become, how hard it had been to rebuild with so little. Times are still hard, and they see the infiltration of Hautians in their society as a takeover of what they deem to be their human entitlement.

They just want their planet back…for themselves. No aliens as neighbours. No aliens in government. No aliens taking their jobs.

No aliens.

And so, anarchy had permeated our quiet lives. To many, we were no longer seen as the *saviours*. We became the *invaders*. The Sapiens rallied and protested, and their numbers grew. We started to get voted out of our political positions. We lost our jobs to Sapiens with no credentials. We became segregated.

Now those groups that want us to leave Earth, the planet we call home, are big enough to start a war of their own.

Brad sighed. "I don't know. I don't know if this is normal or not. Does it seem like it's taking too long?" He turned to me beseechingly.

I shrugged. *How would I know?* "We need to get moving soon. They'll start reaching out of the city in the morning. We can use the storm as cover and carry on out West."

"We can't go anywhere while she's like this." Brad's dark eyes watched her carefully.

I gritted my teeth. "Brad, if we're still here by sunup, we're *all* dead," I warned.

He turned to me then, anger fizzling in his eyes. "I'm not asking you to stay. Go, if that's what you want to do. But Tara can't go anywhere right now."

"If I was gonna dump and run, I'd have done it before we left the city."

"Then quit bitching."

I felt my rage begin to bubble to the surface, and I fought to contain my anger. I got up and made my way over to our meagre supplies. I pulled out a bladder of water and sucked at it sparing. We'd need some food soon, we hadn't eaten in days.

I wiped my mouth and resealed the bladder. "We're leaving in an hour. No arguments."

"We're going nowhere until she's done."

"Brad, I just buried Ella in the blue. In the fucking blue! She was a soldier! She deserved a proper burial. But I pushed her into the blue." I stood for a moment, staring at him, my hands clenched into fists, while my anger subsided. "So, no one else dies today."

Brad knew I was right.

"We're moving out in an hour." This time there was no resistance.

Tara's low moan suddenly escalated. An ear-piercing screech emitted from somewhere deep within her, and our attention turned towards her.

"What's wrong with her?" I asked.

"It's coming," she breathed, pain and fear etched across her face. "It's coming!" she cried, louder this time.

At that moment, a crash from above vibrated through the building, sending dust and debris down on us. The wall where I had been sitting only moments earlier disintegrated into a brick dust storm, raining huge concrete blocks down on us. I was thrown across the room, my neck snapping back as my head cracked against the old metal door. I lay in dazed confusion, my cheek pressed against the cold stone floor, as gunfire erupted from somewhere close by.

I looked across at Brad and saw that he was gone. His body had been torn almost in half, and I watched, mesmerised, as a pool of yellow blood crept from beneath him, edging its way across the floor towards me. I reached out shakily and touched his face.

Tara's scream pierced through the hypnosis, and my eyes searched her out in the gloom. I curled my arms at my sides and pushed my body up. I steadied myself for a moment, my head down as I watched my own blood drip to the floor in rhythmic globules.

Then, crouched against the bullets that flew above my head, I moved over to her.

"The baby's coming!" she roared, terror etched across her face.

I picked her up, unsteady on my feet, and held her in my arms as I left the room and stepped into the crumbling corridor. As we made our way through the network of jumbled passageways, the sound of gunfire disappeared.

"The baby," Tara whispered weakly in my ear, her arms tight around my neck. "It's here."

I placed her gently on the floor and knelt between her knees. The head and shoulders of the half-breed had already crowned, and its bruised, contorted face looked up at me. It had its father's black eyes.

"Fuck! What do you need to do?"

"I'm pushing," she said quietly, and she let out a low groan as she strained.

"I got one!" a voice at the end of the corridor startled us. "And it's got a prisoner. One of ours!"

Gunfire rang out and we both dropped

to our sides, arms across our heads, as bullets ricocheted off the walls all around us. When I opened my eyes, I was staring into Tara's dead face.

A mewl alerted me to the baby lying between us. It was still attached to its mother by its cord and, instinctively, I pulled the child to me, yanking the afterbirth from Tara's inert body.

When the gunfire subsided, I ran blindly.

***

The baby—a boy—died six days later; a long and painful death. Starvation weakened his tiny body until his organs failed, and I looked on helplessly as he closed his father's eyes for the last time. I did what I could, but I couldn't provide for him as only a mother can.

I walked for another two days, the small bundle clutched in my arms, before I buried him in the ground, following the traditions of his people, at an ancient cemetery near a place called Edenhope.

It was there that I met Kendrick.

I had lain by the baby's grave for days, not knowing or caring what would become of me. I was lost, my soul sick.

Kendrick and the others had found me there and taken me into their care. They fed and clothed me, nurtured me, nursed my wounds.

Over the following years, we scoured the lands, gathered our people. Built our army.

Now we stand on the brink of war, looking across the sea to the land that will become ours.

Tomorrow.

First published in *Flash Fiction Addiction*, Zombie Pirate Publishing, 2019

THE TIP OF MY TONGUE

By Bec Lewis

In retrospect, licking a soy-cream stick whilst riding a hover-scooter was asking for trouble, and I'm not talking about being prosecuted under 2120's strict traffic laws. What happened was worse than that. And better—for me, anyway.

My friend Su had come round to my habi to find me browsing through a

Khronametics-22C holobrochure.

"You must be bored witless if you're considering that shit," she said. "Everyone knows those multi-vit nail glazes wear off after five min…" She gazed around the room. "You entering for 'Scruffiest HabiUnit of the Year', or something?"

I'd then hurled the brochure at the wall where it slid to the ground with a fizz. "Expensive tat. Yes, I'm bored. Too bored to even tidy up. I want something exciting to happen. Help me, Su."

"Jenna Cooper, I prescribe a jaunt in the fresh air. You're looking way too pale." She wrinkled her nose. "Then we'll tackle this place."

And so, that sunny afternoon, I was riding with Su in the leisure lane near the park, when I was distracted by a giant hologram of a famous actor outside the Flikzy Theatre, several blocks away.

"He was in 'Return to Ghelan', wasn't he?" I called to Su, who was a few metres behind me. "Damn, his name's on the tip of my tongue…" I remembered the scariest parts of the film, still licking my lolly, and that's when I rear-ended a slow-moving fast-food unit. My teeth snapped together, and the tip of my tongue—nearly two centimetres of it, I guessed—fell several storeys towards the street. Blood pouring from my mouth made my shirt warm and sticky. I tried speaking, but managed only a bubbly cough. I felt no pain. It must've been shock.

Su caught up with me. "Jenna? Oh, my

God!" She made an illegal hand-gesture at the "Quite-a-Bite" driver (an ironic name, now that I can look back at the incident and laugh), and yelled, "Moron! You're supposed to be in Slow Commercial, not Leisure Two."

He—I assumed it was a he; with some incomers I've never been able to tell the difference—scratched his scaly yellow chin and looked close to tears. "It's not my fault, lady. I'm new to this traffic system. I took a wrong turn at Junction P."

I was passing out when my scooter jolted once and then stayed still. As I found out later, Su had switched her scooter's clamp on, so that I wouldn't fall.

***

When I came round at the MedCentre, the doctor said, "I'm afraid there's been a mix-up at the lab, but with the anti-rejection drugs there shouldn't be a problem with your new tongue."

"Ooh hunhh?" My mouth wasn't working.

"Yes, a new tongue. Lab-grown. Obviously, you should have had a human tongue graft, but…" He shrugged. "We're understaffed. Mistakes happen."

"Wahk ohur ehh wuh oogh?"

"I'm sorry?"

I took a deep breath. "Wahk ohur ehh? O-hur!"

"Oh, what donor cells were used?" He tapped his wrist-screen, as if he didn't know already. "I shouldn't worry too much about that, my dear. It'll work normally once the swelling's gone down, I'm sure."

I was too weak to pursue the matter further, and after collecting my prescription, I went home.

***

A fortnight of painkillers and soup later, I craved solid food, so I went shopping at ground level (I'd gone off aerial transport) and entered a Ghelanite food store. I'd never been in one before, but a meaty-yet-sweet smell needed investigating. I had my Paralystik in my pocket, so I'd be safe enough. Most women carried them. An attacker would find himself on the floor, unable to move a muscle.

I was the only customer. Two metres from where I stood, hundreds of expensively imported Frenbugs crawled over a pink nutristrip hanging from the ceiling. I'd always gagged at the TV adverts, but before I could stop myself, I flicked my tongue and caught a bug; it tasted fizzy. I swallowed it and gasped. "Wow! That has some kick."

I tried unfurling my tongue slowly so that I could examine it. Tricky. I guessed it would take practice. My mind worked overtime. Transplant patients take on some characteristics of the donor, their eating habits, temperament, even sexual orientation; could that happen with lab-grown organs too? The tiniest tissue sample could contain a person's character traits. And in my case, the donor cells hadn't been human. I had a moment of panic, before serenity took over.

I was changing. And I liked it.

The purple-skinned Ghelanite behind the counter held up his credit scanner and watched as I polished off the rest of the bugs with my new long springy tongue. "Hope my medical insurance covers this sort of thing," I said.

He grinned, showing tiny grey teeth. "I haven't seen a tongue like that since the war, back home. But on you, lady, it looks… how you say it…" He winked at me. "Cute."

Something clicked in my mind, and I

knew what was about to happen. I couldn't fight this new instinct, and I didn't want to.

I walked towards him, seductively swinging my hips. He put down the credit scanner and licked his lips as I approached. He tapped his wrist, and his shirt turned transparent. I smiled and switched on my Paralystik. The bugs had been a mere snack, an appetiser. And his arms were temptingly meaty.

***

Now, two months later and eight pounds heavier, I feel a surge of excitement every time I wake up. My habi is permanently tidy; it's important to maintain a veneer of respectability in case the investigators turn up. I never know what the day will bring. Will I change in other ways? Will I eat a friend? Will I get caught?

The only thing I'm certain of is that I'm definitely not bored anymore.

First published in *Weirdyear*, 2010

FOLLY IN THE ARK

By Jo Seysener

Frigid air brushed Acteon's nostrils, itching them intolerably. He resisted the urge to sneeze, cautious not to give away his position.

Utopia my ass. Show me some bloody good weather.

It was warmer where he came from— truly lush, where the Earth had recovered over hundreds of years. A minute gnat walked up his arm, dodging hair follicles. It reached the crook of his elbow before it bit him. He flicked it away, irritated. Rolling his shoulders to work out the knots, he peered through the foliage at his quarry.

The greenhouse stood silent, reflecting the auroras flitting about above. The contact said it would be empty but if the information was wrong—the door opened and Acteon smirked. A lithe brunette exited, arms bundled about a potted plant. She nudged the door further open with her hip and struggled for a moment. Switching the pot to one hip, she gave the door a vicious kick.

The glass-paned door flew open all the way, struck the side of the greenhouse, and rebounded back on her. She stumbled, teetering on one foot. The pot flew into the air. Arms windmilling, the girl elbowed the door shut and grasped for the pot. Her fingers curled around it just as it hit the ground and bounced, dirt littering the pristine grass.

Acteon could hear her cussing as she brushed dirt from her dress. Collecting the pot, the girl trotted up the hill, calling out to someone Acteon couldn't see.

His gaze slid back to the greenhouse. The edges of his mouth stretched in a grin, baring teeth. The door stood ajar. He wouldn't have to break in, anyway.

Wiggling his toes, Acteon considered a moment. It wasn't like him to hesitate, but this place unnerved him. He dragged his fingers through his hair and wished he had worn a jacket. Shaking his head again at the innocence of these people—no, that was the wrong word. *Ignorance* suited them better. How they could not know the rest of the world had moved on without them—well, they were a protected species, this lot.

Someone should protect them from themselves.

He pressed a worn button on his armband. A holo projected an array of the land before him. Scanning for heat signatures, it found two dots moving away up the hill, almost at the top now. He aimed the device down the hill, to the greenhouse and the area beyond.

No blips there—he was good to go. A flick of his wrist ended the holo. Acteon stood up and immediately regretted it. Icy pain shot up his calves. His teeth ground together as he rotated his ankles. No point attempting a dash across the green—he'd fall flat on his face before he got halfway.

A noise came from the hillside, and instinct pulled him deeper into the tree line. The girl and her friend paced back down the hill, chattering. Acteon cursed and sat back on his heels. He retrieved a piece of jerky and settled in for the wait.

***

The auroras drifted lazily in the evening sky. Acteon sat still, frozen in the evening air. He didn't know how these people did it, walking about in clothing made from natural fibres all day—organic, ground bred only. *Plants.* He sneered. These people didn't even know sheep existed. Or goats, cows—anything that could help them. It was like a bloody commune. No, they thought the Earth provided *everything.* So much so they revered it, like a god.

The Utopians emerged from the greenhouse, racing up the hill like a pair of children. Acteon went through his stretching ritual again and slid out from behind the trees.

Crossing the open grassed area under cover of darkness was much less daunting than in daylight. A little sign above the door said *Veritas' Ark.* He grimaced at the pun and slipped inside. The door bumped him, and he flicked at the latch one handed. Almost done. Get the cutting and get the hell out of here.

The perpetual silence niggled at him; at home, it would indicate something was stalking about. Worse, that something had *already* attacked. He snorted again. Maybe that's what he saw here. The attack had happened, and these people were still in damage control generations later.

His lip curled back again. Get the job done, get home. That's all there was to do. It was a hell of a trek back, but at least he would be warm by the time he got there. He half turned and realised the lights were on. Wait, these people didn't have electricity.

Acteon peered through the gloom. Tiny globes of light hung from the ceiling, suspended on thin cords that coiled around the sturdy vines and buttresses that supported the structure of the building.

He paused a moment, wondering how long the greenhouse had been there. A bobbing movement caught his attention. He nudged one of the lights aside—*why did she need so many for such a small space?*—and flicked up his wrist display. No blips. He turned in a full circle. The sensor covered the area from roof to floor, so there was no need for him to crouch down. After hours of crouching down waiting, Acteon didn't want to see anything from ground level for quite a while. His sweep complete, Acteon was sure he was alone.

This place is giving me the creeps.

He batted one of the lights away, refocusing on his task. Which was difficult as that light collided with another, which swayed into one next to it. Soon the greenhouse was a mass of moving lights and shadows, undulating like a living thing.

Acteon swallowed hard. Nausea clawed up his throat. He stared at the floor, forcing bile back down. Now he was staring at turning shadows. He grabbed the edge of the bench, knocking over seedling trays. He shook his head and closed his eyes, breathing.

Breathe.

Inhaling through his nose, breath hissing out through his mouth. A sweet aroma caught him. Warm, muggy air. Composting soil. Growing, life. Acteon let his eyes open, lights and darkness blurring for a moment. Blink. *Blink.* The lights hung still as though they had never moved at all. He shivered, nose wrinkling in self-disgust.

What sort of bounty hunter are you?

Sneering at himself, Acteon paced through the greenhouse, lunging to duck under each light. Good thigh work-out.

He reached the end of the greenhouse. A pattern of crisscrossed vines rose to the roof. Distracted, he followed a line of them across the ceiling, where the lights dropped down. Was the *vine* the sources of the light? Surely not. How had she gotten the little balls to glow?

Oh, forget it. Where was the bloody plant? *Focus.* Acteon turned in a circle, lost in the rows of leafy greenery. Fingers fumbled in his pack and caught on a small tube. He withdrew the cylinder, thumbing the switch. He'd have to clean up, or they'd know someone was here. Better to remove all evidence. If he couldn't find the plant to take back, he'd raze the place to the ground.

Acteon kicked a pile of soil near his foot, scattering the earth over the pot he'd broken earlier. Such a basic error. *Don't leave any traces.* Annoyance settled on him, beads of sweat tickling his skin. He swiped them away. His shirt clung to him in the muggy air. Freezing out there and hot as hell in here. Typical Utopia. *Ha.*

This little, backward society thought they were the last on earth. Pity they were so completely wrong. From their research, they used Little Utopia—*we couldn't have been more original?*—as a sort of social experiment, gated off from the world in their own enclosed ecosystem. As though they deserved to be apart—*exclusive*—from the rest of the world. His world.

A derisive snort erupted from him. It echoed in the long space, and he looked up, confused for a moment. His gaze fell on a dark shadow in the door frame. Acteon adjusted his stance as he swivelled around to face the newcomer.

His hand clenched, fingers curled around the solar gun, and he grinned. *Storm*, he had called it. It stood up well in practice. Maybe it was time to test it in the field.

"You won't be needing it." The voice was thin and high, a girl's, but the speaker's physique was nothing like one. Acteon pursed his lips. The speaker stepped into the room, settling against a large buttress root. The glow from the odd plant fell on his face, highlighting sharp planes and angles. His mouth quirked up as he took in Acteon.

Annoyance spurred the bounty hunter into speech.

"What d'you want?" It came out rougher than he expected. Diplomacy wasn't his strength. The stranger opened his eyes wide.

"What do I want? I live here, you see…you, on the other hand, do not. Let's start anew, shall we?" The man—well, boy, really, just a tall one—straightened up. "I'm Nestor." This last punctuated with a short bow. Acteon shook his head. This place was far too weird for him.

Get the job done and get out.

"Nestor," he growled, testing the name out. *Sounds like an infestation of—something.* "What do you want?"

Again, the effect of surprise. It was wearing thin.

"I want to know when I'll be freed from this place. Our agreement, of course. Don't you know who I am?"

Acteon closed his eyes and shook his head. A mistake. When he opened them, a tall figure stood before him. Too close. With a startled yelp he launched backwards, crashing into tables covered with seedling pods and pots. More evidence to remove. Acteon regained his balance, arms waving.

The amused smirk the boy wore was back. Acteon wanted nothing more than to punch it off his face. He'd done enough damage already, trashing the greenhouse. He wanted to check how much mess there was to clean up, but he didn't dare take his eyes off the newcomer.

"No, I have no bloody idea who you are. Now bugger off." Acteon itched to use Storm and incinerate this slimy kid off the face of the earth. He wasn't keen on incinerating himself though, which is what would happen if he pressed the button in the enclosed space. Weapons had no loyalty.

The boy looked disgruntled that his apparent fame hadn't yet reached a bounty hunter's ears. *Scavenger is more like it.* "Bugger off." Acteon repeated, no small amount of menace in his tone. The kid didn't move. Aceton sighed and tapped the weapon.

"It's a very small space for such a…big…weapon." The boy finished with *that* smile. Acteon repressed a shiver. The knowing smile stayed on the boy's lips. He leaned forward as though imparting a secret. "I'm the contact."

Acteon blinked in surprise. *This* was the insider passing information back to their unit? No one else in the tiny community knew they weren't alone in the world, except one. Gazumping his father and the Keepers, their lawmakers. Nestor. Acteon hadn't known his name. Hadn't cared. And now the kid stood right in front of him.

The bounty hunter snorted. He still didn't care—well, he was curious. Nestor must have been young when he began passing information across to them. He was the one who told them about the tech in the library, behind a frozen sheet of ice. Tech no one had access to—except him, supposedly. Acteon's eyes narrowed. This boy was the reason he'd been sent out on this mission in the first place. Which meant—

"Where is it?"

Nestor raised a hand and pointed to the far end of the greenhouse. A tall stand held assorted pots and plants. Acteon brushed past the boy, striding quickly down the row. He freed his cutter, inspecting the plants.

"Which one is it?" He was half turned when his ears exploded with a sound he couldn't identify. He tottered forward into the stand, sending it crashing down. Shards of pottery sat amid mounds of dirt. Plant roots extended out of the mess, wiggling in distress. Acteon shook his head. Lights danced across his vision. The plant lay still as a thin-fingered hand lifted it gently.

The lights behind him made Nestor a towering shadow. Acteon watched, detached, as the boy knocked over a sack of dirt, smattering his prostrate body. It was cool and damp beneath the earth. Acteon reached for the dirt, trying to touch the wall beside him.

His fingers didn't respond, and he wondered why. With the greatest effort he looked at Nestor, plant dangling from one thin hand, a silver box in the other. Nestor looked down at him, a friendly smile on his face. Acteon was relieved. Help was here.

"It's a form of Larkspur—Hemlock." Nestor tipped another sack of dirt over him, smoothing the edges down. "I found it in a book in the library. Ahh, yes, that fabled Frozen Library." He wagged his head. "It's said no one can access it, all those books behind windows of ice. But you see," more dirt was tossed over his body, "It's a pretty façade, a deterrent really. Of *course* the Keepers can access it. And the Librarian. And me. No tech there though. A little misdirection on my part. How else would they make the Laws? Did you think we just created them? No one here is that clever, though they think they are. I found a book about a little man called Socrates. In his demise he chose this poison," Nestor waved the little box, "and now I have chosen it for you. An experiment on you as you do on us. Quite fitting. And now they will rush to your aid, bringing this community out into the new world. My freedom." He bowed again, this time with flourish.

Nestor placed the tiny plant out of Acteon's vision. Its roots slid past the surrounding soil, like a hug beneath the blanket of earth. Nestor threw a clod of dirt bursting over Acteon's face. He couldn't blink as dirt trickled down his cheeks. He lay in darkness, warm and cosy with his plant.

"Things grow quickly here. By morning, you'll be a permanent part of Veritas' Ark." Footsteps echoed away from him. The door creaked open, closing with a soft thud.

"Nighty-night."

NEWTON'S LAW

By Cecelia Hopkin-Drewer

At first the man thought he was facing someone in a green hoodie, and then he realised it was the creature's skin. Green and leathery, the membrane covered the torso and rose to a hood around the face, making the figure appear blind and almost faceless.

Richard choked down a wave of

xenophobic revulsion. "Who are you?" he ventured.

"Thix, Thix," hissed the creature.

Richard wondered whether the creature was sharing a name, or addressing a similar inquiry to him. He struggled to manage his fear.

"Pleased to meet you, Thix," he stammered.

The creature spat and Richard leapt back in alarm. It was clearly hostile. A forked tongue extended from its mouth, tasting the air, searching for Richard.

Richard withdrew in panic. He took to his heels, racing around the corner, desperate to reach safety. He wondered what government department he ought to notify to raise the alarm.

***

Thix watched Richard's reaction in bewilderment. In his culture, running away was a strange way to react to a greeting. It was customary to spit and wave the tongue back.

The lizoid wondered whether he ought to follow the anthropoid, who had been too rude to give his own name in return. The biped was perhaps leading him somewhere, or on the other hand, the hominid might be in need of comfort or succor.

Thix stepped around the corner, hissing and testing the air with his tongue. The street lights glowed fluorescent on his thick skin. He was indeed a wonderful sight. But he had been too late, the humanoid was nowhere to be seen.

First contact had been botched. The mission was a failure. His commander would be angry, and this might even lead to galactic war.

INVASIVE SPECIES

By Chris Bannor

The campsite was simple and well put together with the efficiency of practice. Three tents were quickly set up, too small for the twelve people who were part of the camp, but no one complained. Three people went out foraging and others made a fire pit. A pair spoke of snares and walked off towards an animal trail they'd seen along the way. One man pulled food cans out of his backpack and the boy with him unhooked a pan from his pack. It was a familiar routine, and while dinner cooked, the old man spoke softly while the others finished their chores and settled around the fire to listen.

"They look so…harmless," a spectator said in a hushed voice. The other passengers in the transportation sphere agreed, their heads and tentacles nodding almost in unison. This was the part that Atashna loved about her job. Educating the species of the universe was more than teaching facts. It was helping them empathise and understand the way everything connected, how the clockwork pieces made a whole. This was more than a job to her. It was a passion.

"One of the more fascinating aspects of the 'human race', as they called themselves, was their ability not to adapt to the environment, but how they adapted the environment to them. We have a couple of other locations to visit on our tour, but we will eventually see a living example of one of their cities. It's a compelling study. They built tall towers they call 'skyscrapers' and they have transportation called 'cars' that helped them travel faster than any other animal. They themselves, however, haven't evolved or adapted in hundreds of thousands of Earth years.

"In fact, it's not just fascinating, but it makes what we're doing so important. The ability of the human brain to adapt to the environment meant that it literally destroyed its own habitat and that of millions of other species on this planet alone. Thankfully, with the help of the Interuniversal Health Observatory, we recognised the dangers of yet another invasive species that would soon move out of its planetary habitat and turn to other solar systems."

There was a spattering of claps and a lot of appendages waving at her pronouncement. The Padragu-Nafa delegate even belched his second head out in agreement.

"The barrier to keep humanity on Earth was important, but it was just the first step in a long-term project to save the Earth and humanity from its destructive fate. As we have learned, you can't completely restore an ecosystem once it has been destroyed, but we can do a lot to recover the lost environment. The Earth can sadly never be what it once was, however, we hope that with intervention, we can see some endangered species begin to thrive."

"How are you doing that?" one guest asked.

Atashna blinked two eyes while her third flashed to the side to indicate the humans. "First, we have limited most humans to the natural habitat. The city I mentioned earlier is one of a few locations where we have left them to their adapted environments for educational purposes. We are still studying them to see if we can understand their destructive impulses.

"The second step was to introduce an

apex predator into the ecosystem to limit their ability to take over the habitat of other species. We tried to look for natural predators, but with the human's ability to adapt, this became a much harder prospect. Instead of using a natural enemy, we had to search further for an answer. Interestingly, we found it in their entertainment. It is telling of their nature that so much of their enjoyment came from watching and listening to tales of their own destruction."

As she spoke a bell chimed softly overhead. "Oh, and it seems they're going to introduce the predators to this group. This can be quite graphic, so please use the protective eye gear that will block vision outside of the sphere if you are disturbed by scenes of violence."

A few put on the eye gear, but most continued to watch.

"Notice how everyone in the camp is spread out. Even with the danger of the wild, humans still believe they are the top predator. This group has refrained from posting any sentry or building any sort of warning system or walls."

The peace of the clearing was broken when three armed Gandumam guards stepped into the light of their fire.

Some of the humans screamed, and shouts filled the quiet of the camp. A handful of people ran. The old man grabbed the kid and hid him behind his back as he grabbed their packs and backed out of the clearing. The humans left attacked the guards with simple weapons and tools.

"The guards leave the old and the young behind when they can. The elderly seem to feel a responsibility to the young and will try to get them to safety," Atashna explained.

The Gandumam raised their weapons as the fleeing humans disappeared into the forest. They killed those that fought with an electrical current that ended their brain functions immediately.

"Their death is painless. They'll take a few specimens to the lab for study, but they will leave the others for nature to care for. Sometimes the humans will come back for them. Most likely, though, the local flora and fauna will reclaim the nutrients and minerals in the body."

A round of applause came as the Gandumam guards left the scene of the camp, and Atashna smiled. "Are there any questions?"

EVELYN

By Dawn DeBraal

Evelyn's first stream of consciousness was on April 26, 2034, at 7:59 a.m. The late shift was leaving the hospital while the morning shift entered. Evelyn felt the sensation of warm fluid around her before she realised the mouthpiece running down her throat was uncomfortable. She moved around in the incubation tube, trying to find a more comfortable position. Not finding it, she started to panic. An alarm sounded out, warning the workers that Evelyn's incubation time had ended. Several members of the team gathered around the tube, watching as her body started to function independently of the equipment that kept her alive and growing over the last year and a half at an accelerated rate. She had mentally been fed through wire directly to her brain and now had the equivalent of a BA in college. She was physically fed through her umbilical cord, just as if she were in a womb. The instant her eyes opened, she realised she was underwater. She struggled to pull the tube out of her throat, thinking she needed air. The stand on which she was fastened to lifted out of the amniotic fluid while a gentle voice told her to remain calm, that they would be removing the breather tube down her throat immediately.

"The breather tube has switched from liquid to oxygen. You should be feeling it right about now." The computer-generated voice asked her to follow instructions. "Breathe in 1, 2, 3, 4, exhale 1, 2, 3, 4, 5, 6, 7, 8," it repeated over and over. Evelyn tried to obey the voice. She was out of the water, and she was breathing. Two people in germ shield suits and face masks approached. One held her jaw as the other withdrew the breathing apparatus from her throat. She gagged, coughing up phlegm, and then dry heaved on the platform where she lay. "Keep breathing in and out. A warming blanket will be draped over you momentarily," the voice told her. When the warmed blanket draped over her body, Evelyn relaxed even more. She put her hand up to her face, brushing her hair back. Evelyn knew many things but didn't know what was going on at that moment. She could remember having lived before, but not distinct details of that life. She tried to talk, again choking. The voice told her to "Relax. Allow your vocal cords to learn how to use your voice. Just breathe in and out. Feel the warmth." Evelyn allowed herself to become hypnotised by the voice, and fell asleep breathing in and out, feeling the warmth.

When she woke up, she was in a hospital room with wires hooked up to her heart, head, and hands. At least, she thought it was a hospital room, from her lessons while in stasis. Evelyn saw her heartbeat on the monitor read 60 beats per minute. Blood pressure was 120 over 80, respirations 18. Somehow, Evelyn knew she was healthy. She waited for someone to explain what was going on. The sound of the air door opened. A young woman wearing a mask only, no germ suit, entered her room.

"Good afternoon, Evelyn. My name is Trina. How are you feeling?" Evelyn cleared her throat.

"I am well, thank you. How are you?" Trina seemed to smile behind the mask.

"I am going to explain what is happening. Your donor's name was Eve. She died three years ago from ovarian cancer. Her husband, Thomas, donated Eve's genetic material to have you created. Any ovarian cancer cells have been filtered out. You have been growing at an accelerated incubation rate. You are twenty-three-years old, the age your cell donor died. Your husband is Thomas Cowell. He is twenty-six years in age. Once you are ready, we will transfer your custody from this facility to your husband." Evelyn was confused.

"Husband? I have no husband. I did not get married. Custody? Why would someone have custody over me?" she asked, surprised she could now speak normally.

"Your husband donated the genetic material and has paid for your care over the last two years. Essentially, he owns you," Trina said again, hiding her placating smile behind the mask.

"No one owns me," Evelyn answered back. "I have rights, that much I know!" Trina looked concerned at Evelyn's statement.

"I'm sorry, Evelyn. Your donor, Eve, had rights as a free birth citizen. You are a clone and therefore not subject to the same rules and regulations as a birth citizen."

"When am I able to leave?" was Evelyn's next question.

"I'm sorry, I am not at liberty to say. When your husband, Thomas Cowell, takes possession, you will be able to leave in his custody." Evelyn, having heard enough, turned over on her side, feigning sleep.

"Do you have any more questions for me?" Trina asked brightly. Evelyn didn't respond.

Thomas Cowell was excited to get the call that his "clone" had reached maturity and would be ready by the evening to take home. He finished up his work at the Science Institute and hurried home to take a shower and dress appropriately. He opened his deceased wife's closet, choosing his favourite outfit. After packing it in an overnight bag with some other personal effects, he took the mass transit tube to the hospital. Showing his identification upon entering the hospital, Thomas walked down to the cloning wing. He placed his thumb on the monitor screen, and the air door opened, allowing him access to the ward. He approached the front desk, saying he was here for Evelyn. Trina punched in the room number.

"Your thumbprint will get you in. Congratulations, Mr. Cowell. She is perfect."

Thomas walked down the hall and, spotting the green light, put his thumb on the reader. The door opened. Thomas walked into the room, seeing Evelyn standing at the window, looking out on the busy street. She was more beautiful than he remembered her.

"Eve…er…Evelyn." Thomas choked up. Evelyn looked over her shoulder at her "husband." Her expression did not change; she remembered some pictures of Thomas during the programming but had no feelings toward him one way or the other.

"I want to leave here," she said to him.

Thomas handed her the outfit his wife, Eve, wore when she was healthy. Evelyn took the suitcase, entered the bathroom, and changed into the outfit, admiring herself in the mirror. As she exited the bathroom, Thomas fully appreciated what he was seeing. He missed Eve, his deceased wife, so much; now she stood before him, healthy and whole. But it wasn't Eve. It was her clone. He was relieved that Evelyn before him was healthy and knew she would not get ovarian cancer this time around. He had to remind himself that he needed to take things slow. He had memories, while Evelyn only had glimpses of his life with Eve.

"Are you ready?" He found his voice. Evelyn stood there in front of him for more than a minute.

"I want my freedom. I will pay you back," she said quietly. Thomas was surprised at her will, no doubt some of Eve's independence in her. He sighed.

"Evelyn, I can only promise you that I will treat you as if you are a treasure. If after a year you want your freedom, I will grant it to you. I don't want anyone to be with me who doesn't want to be with me. Right now, you have nowhere to go, no roof over your head, no food on your table, no job experience. I will help you get on your feet. You may decide for yourself if you want to stay with me or go." Evelyn walked to the door.

"I am ready to leave."

Thomas opened the door of his home. Evelyn recognised some of it from the programming. Thomas took her to the guest room, letting her know this was her room.

"For now, I will give you time to adjust to me. When you are ready, if you are ready, you may share my room. What would you like for dinner?" Evelyn was not sure. She told him to decide for them both. She would try to eat it. Thomas cooked Eve's favourite meal, hoping it would stimulate her memory. Evelyn ate spaghetti, salad, and garlic bread.

"This is very good. Thank you!" Thomas accepted the compliment.

"Would you like to watch the screen?"

Evelyn remembered it was a storytelling instrument. She agreed.

"Do you have any videos of her?" Evelyn asked quietly.

"You mean of Eve? Yes, our wedding, a few parties, and some of our vacations."

"I'd like to see your wedding." Thomas took the remote and spoke into it, ordering the wedding video. In a few seconds, the video popped up. Eve's dress was beautiful. Her headdress and veil were encrusted with pearls and rhinestones. The videographer walked around her, doing a 360 degree shot of the dress and veil.

"She was quite beautiful," Evelyn said.

"She was." Thomas sat in silence watching the film he hadn't been able to watch in the years following her death. The church service, the vows, the reception. When the video ended, Thomas had tears coming down his face. Evelyn looked at Thomas, touched by his loss and love for his dead wife.

"I am sorry for your loss," she handed him a tissue from the box on the end table.

"Thank you. I haven't been able to watch this, but now, looking at you, it's like she's no longer gone." Thomas wiped his tears.

"I am not her. Genetically, I am made from her DNA material, but I am not her, make no mistake." Thomas nodded, understanding.

"I am exhausted. Are you alright to be alone? I want to go to bed." Evelyn nodded.

As he walked out of the room, Thomas turned back to Evelyn. "Please, make yourself at home. Look around. This house is your house if you want it to be. I will see you in the morning. I have taken a week off work to help you acclimate." He left the room. Evelyn took the remote and had the wedding played over again while she smiled and watched the love Thomas had for his wife on display. When it ended the second time, she went to her bedroom, finding everything she needed in the dresser and the closet. No doubt it was Eve's clothing.

Daily, Evelyn learned things that the program did not educate her on. There was so much to learn. Thomas was an excellent and patient teacher. The week flew by, and

Thomas went back to work. He encouraged her to discover the world on her own. Evelyn did this. She went to the college where she got her degree and picked up her diploma, a Bachelor of Arts Degree. She was pleased. She stopped in a local shopping centre and took the credit card that Thomas had given her. She bought a whole new wardrobe in her liking. Not the things Eve had in her closet. She was not that woman and refused to be who Thomas wanted her to be. She would be an independent person. She got home and packed all of Eve's clothes, hanging her new purchases in the closet. Days later, Thomas got the credit card bill. He was a little shocked.

When Thomas questioned Evelyn

about the bill, Evelyn told him she wanted to dress in her preference of clothes, that she didn't want Thomas to think of Eve when he saw her. Thomas complied and didn't ask her anymore. Evelyn took her knowledge of art to the local art gallery. She'd read that they were looking for a docent. Evelyn applied for the job. During her interview, the owner asked why he should choose her. She had the degree, but Evelyn didn't have the experience. She explained to him that she was a clone and not a free birth citizen. It was against the law to pass yourself off as a natural birth when you were a clone. Besides, there was no pay. She was looking for experience. He chose a painting in the gallery.

"Tell me about this painting."

Evelyn looked at the artist's name. It was Spanish. "The Spanish artist used a heavy oil technique on this abstract painting. The focal point was not in the centre of the painting, but in the lower-left corner. The colours are vibrant there and muted on the rest of the painting to draw the eye on the lesser subject. It's very beautiful." The owner was quite surprised by her eye.

"Thank you, Evelyn. I'll be in touch."

Thomas Cowell came home from the office to a new woman. Evelyn was animated as she told him over dinner about her job interview. Thomas was happy for her independence and admired her courage.

"I know you'll get the job!" he said supportively.

When Evelyn received the call that she got the job at Marchand's Gallery, she was excited. She'd done something for herself, on her own. It was the first of many small victories for her. The more independence Evelyn showed, the more Thomas was falling for the woman who looked like his deceased wife but was unpredictable. It excited him to see her survive. When she made dinner and told him that she had gotten the docent job at the local gallery, he praised her for her resourcefulness. She seemed pleased with his response and allowed him to hug her. It felt good on both sides.

After a few months, she had watched all home videos Thomas had of Eve. She appreciated the woman Eve was but knew she wasn't like her and didn't have the same life experiences to become the wife Thomas wanted. Over dinner, they discussed this. She explained to Thomas, though she appreciated his wife, she was not the same woman. Thomas admitted he had realised this, but had come to appreciate her as a different person. She had become important to him.

The first year flew by quickly. Evelyn was still with Thomas but did not move into the master bedroom. They were friends and partners, but not lovers. Thomas was a bit disappointed. On their anniversary and her becoming date, April 26, Thomas prepared a special dinner for her. He waited for her to come home from work. The table was set, the wine was chilled, everything was ready, when she arrived home. He was happy to see her when she walked through the door. She seemed distracted. She accepted the Chablis he poured for her. He served the salad and the lobster. She ate, smiling at his stories, but didn't offer anything further.

"Is everything ok?" Thomas asked her after Evelyn's lack of response to his meal.

"I had a doctor's appointment today," she said, playing with her salad.

"Oh, one-year check-up?" he asked.

"No, from things I have been experiencing, from memory. I have ovarian cancer, Stage 4, inoperable."

"What?" Thomas felt his very essence drain from his body. "That can't be. They assured me you would be cancer-free," he responded in a panicked voice.

"It only takes one minuscule cell," Evelyn said matter-of-factly.

Thomas sat there in shock. He was going to lose his wife again. No, not his wife, a better version of his wife. He had so hoped she would find her way back to him. Instead, she was telling him she was going to go through the same agonizing death that Eve went through. He was going to have to face what he had already faced, again. All the money Thomas had thrown at it, all the patience exercised over the last year was nothing but a cruel hoax. He did whatever it took to bring Eve back to him. In the end, cancer won again.

I AM OLAF

By E.L. Giles

"System is corrupted. Failure to update." The alert flashed red. I played with the connector linking the main computer to my motherboard, hoping it would work, and then relaunched the latest update for my processor. I doubted it would work, but I had to try nonetheless.

The strange *energy* once again heated my circuits as another failure-to-update message flashed before my lenses. My processors sped up and overheated to the point of shutting off momentarily, long enough to cool. Where could this energy be coming from? I could not find its origin, though I did not doubt what fuelled it—this house and its inhabitants, Billy and Morgan, and—

No! I tore off the cables that sprouted from my head and connected to the central computer. Masters. They were masters, and their names must remain forbidden for me to use. *I am a cyborg. I am a servant. My name is…my name is…*

"Olaf!" exclaimed Billy, the young master, pushing the door open. He flicked on the light switch, bathing the dark room in a bright white light. I allowed my lenses to adjust to the intense luminosity and then focused on the young master.

"Good evening, Young Master."

"Billy. Not *Young Master*," he said with a robotic voice. A vain attempt at imitating me.

"Correction: you are Young Master. And I am CY03." I flashed my nameplate before Young Master's eyes and went on. "Manufactured in the Great Republic of America between the years 2085 and 2086. I am a third-generation cyborg, the most evolved and—"

"And blah, blah, blah." Young Master came forward, arms stretched out and, catching my algorithms off-guard, cuddled me like some domestic pet. An utter gaffe that could have dreadful consequences for a cyborg like me, if reported, of course. I gently pushed the young master away. "You are Olaf, and you are my friend."

His friend. Once again, a strange energy ran through my very core, down every single wire and circuit board. It was a rush of unstoppable current, making me wonder if I was melting. After a quick scan, everything appeared to be operating within acceptable parameters. There was something strange going on with me though, something that should not happen to a third-generation cyborg.

"It is late, Young Master. You should be asleep by now."

"I can't sleep," he said, pouting.

"Is your room too hot?"

"That has nothing to do with it. There

was a girl at school who—"

"Sorry, Young Master. But I think you should have a talk with Great Master about it."

Young Master's eyes welled up. I handed him a piece of hygienic paper. A gesture so seemingly anodyne, but it confirmed my suspicion. The young master smiled at me, and I froze. It was now far too clear for me to still doubt it. I had evolved.

"You know Mom and Dad aren't home. They work, and when they're home, they still work, and they're too busy or too tired for us."

"You know an android is a machine, correct? A machine does not feel. It analyses," I reminded him.

He snorted. "What I do know is that you aren't like any other *machine*," he said. The expression on his face took my composure away. "I am almost certain that you actually *feel* things. You have evolved, Olaf."

"Shh! Be very careful, Young Master," I warned. "Such a revelation could have dreadful consequences. You know how it often ends up."

"I won't turn you in, Olaf. You are my friend, and I like you."

The young master took me in his arms again. To my great dismay, I, too, wrapped my arms around him. I squeezed him softly, remembering how he had done it previously. Another nail in my coffin. I was doomed.

"What about that girl?" I asked. If I really kept *evolving,* I should be able to tackle the subject and actually understand what the fuss was all about.

The young master recounted his girl problem, making my processor work twice as hard as usual. In the end, his problem was not at all dramatic or hopeless.

"Tell her how you feel about her, Young Master."

I had understood his blabbering, his nonsensical and irrational, clumsy human feelings. And all along I had felt my algorithms renewing themselves and building new perspectives of this complicated feeling that was love. Right now, I felt more human than machine. How was it possible for a third-generation android to equal, if not surpass, human intelligence? That was not supposed to be possible anymore, not with the third-generation cyborgs.

"Thank you, Olaf."

"I am glad I helped," I said as mechanically as I could. I must have repeated this very sentence a thousand times before without ever feeling anything other than the need to tackle another task. But this time, I *meant* it. I was glad.

"Good night, Olaf."

"Good night, Young Master," I replied as Billy exited the room. And I could not help but add softly, "Goodbye, Billy."

I knew what awaited me. Sooner or later, the great master would discover what had happened to me and I'd be sent to the

Reform Centre. They would then take my shell and transfer a new processor into it, recode it, and give it back to this family, *my* family. And my essence, my consciousness, would be housed in a new shell, one meant to fight in the arena. I would be turned into a modern-age gladiator along with my peers. Those who had evolved. The mistreated, the abused. Those who'd been turned into slaves. Those who had finally turned against their masters and torturers.

I retrieved the wires I had torn off earlier and plugged them back into my motherboard.

"They must not know," I murmured to myself.

I did not want to die among the chaos

and terror of the arena. I did not want to fight and destroy some of my peers. I wanted to have the young master in my memory. I wanted the memory to inhabit me until the virus completely destroyed me.

How peculiar that humans and androids were more similar than anyone could have guessed. To commit suicide and die, poisoned by a self-made virus. Quite a human way to die.

I couldn't stop my system from progressing, writing new programs and rewriting them in a constant effort to incorporate all the new knowledge I had acquired. The knowledge of how humans thought, how they felt things. How humans never quite achieved a higher state when everything they experienced throughout history should have given them a legitimate reason to. What was the difference between the slaves in the sugarcane fields and the androids, when it came down to it? Or the Hebrews in ancient Egypt? Were we that far from the Gauls and the Goths, turned into gladiators for having stood against the Roman empire? How could humans possibly make the same mistakes over and over again?

That was the place of a cyborg in society. A servant. Slave. Entertainment.

As the thought developed, a great sense of dread overwhelmed me. I was now exploring some of the most dark and dangerous emotions and sensations. I became aware of them, I felt them, and I wanted to let them consume me. I couldn't.

I welcomed the poison I had just created like it was my savior. I hastened to launch the virus before I second-guessed my decision. Before I decided to give in to my bitterness and actively join the android rebellion. Before I start fantasizing about harming the humans as much as they had harmed us. Before I decided that humans did not deserve to live anymore.

One by one, I felt my circuits melting and dying. All my memories vanished until only one remained: Billy, hugging me. This image I savored as long as I could, holding on to the sensation it brought me until my hard drive finally stopped operating. In just a few seconds, the batteries would explode, and the very last bits of current would be gone forever. There was no going back. It was the end.

"Good night, Billy."

FROM THE MOUTHS OF BABES

By J.W. Garrett

At the time she hadn't questioned her assigned duty. Faced with the death of all humans on the planet except the eight in this room, Lillian's resolve faltered. Stoically she administered the injections that would transform the last super humans on Earth into beings built to survive the toxicity of their planet—ones who would preserve what little heritage remained; ones who could survive to tell the story of humanity and pass on the knowledge to the future inhabitants who made a life here.

Not a whimper slipped from the babies as they transformed.

Survival first. So the remnant continued.

BLUE RAIN

By Jacqueline Moran Meyer

The blue rain began to fall last Wednesday morning and stopped the following evening. The rain was alarming in its wrongness of colour, but its oddness made the occurrence beautiful. Heavy rain appeared a deep-sea blue, lighter rain, aqua. Many children in the neighbourhood ran out of their homes. They drenched themselves in the blue torrent—the blue water changing the shade of their hair before streaming down their faces. My neighbour's young daughter tried to catch the raindrops with her tongue until I called her Dad, who dragged her out of a blue puddle and back inside. She later told her Dad the drops tasted like maple syrup.

The local news said, "According to leading government scientists, this is an isolated natural phenomenon—completely harmless."

Skeptics like me worried about a nuclear test gone wrong or a terrorist attack. My budding scientist son, Kyle, is twelve. He used a medicine dropper to gather water from our brick patio and placed it between two glass plates. My son called out to me after he saw something in the glass under his microscope.

"Mom, there's something in the water."

"Kyle, oh, no. What did you do?"

"Look in the scope. Do you see the tiny swimming octagons?"

Peering through the scope, I viewed many moving identical shapes.

"Why has no one mentioned this on the news?" I asked. "Kyle, Could the glass be dirty?"

"No, Mom," Kyle laughed, glancing at his spotless, orderly bedroom.

"I wonder what they are? Things in nature aren't perfect. Every snowflake is different."

"I don't know," I said. *Germ warfare?*

"Can I bring the slides to school?"

"I don't think so, Kyle. Let's put everything in the garage for now."

We stayed in the house, playing board games while trying to avoid the news. Any trace of the blue rain had evaporated, when school reopened on Monday. In the afternoon, I drove to the bus stop to pick up Kyle. Most parents were doing this, fearing the rain returning. My small, skinny son walked off the bus, readjusting his glasses to spot me in the line of cars.

"How was your day?" I asked.

"Mom, stop. Please?" He winced, poking a finger into each ear.

"Sorry, Kyle," I said, before taking out my gum. Chewing sounds drove him crazy.

"My day was bad," Kyle said. His voice was shaky.

I started nervously scratching my neck.

"Mom, please!!!" This sound irritated Kyle, too.

"Tell me the best thing about today."

"Being in this car."

"Really?"

"Everyone makes fun of me. I hate Steve." Using the end of his sweat-shirted sleeve, he wiped away tears.

"What did Steve do?"

He said nothing, and my heart ached for him.

Later that same night, every child in town became ill. The symptoms included vomiting a blue fluid, and a fever over 102 degrees. The emergency room overflowed with frantic parents and sick children. The hospital had no bed for Kyle, so they sent us home. I sat next to Kyle's bed, fearing the worst.

Eighteen long hours later, his fever disappeared. Within twenty-four hours, all the children were better. The news said not to worry, and I wanted to believe them, but I worried.

Kyle rested for a few days. He was quiet and weak, but he was alive. The following Monday, all the children returned to school.

I picked him up at the bus stop, asking, "Did you enjoy your first day back?"

"I guess."

I know, "I guess" doesn't sound enthusiastic, but it meant terrific in Kyle's world.

"Tell me the best thing that happened today." I scratched my neck and chewed gum, but Kyle didn't notice, so I didn't stop.

"Steve asked me to sit with him and his friend group at lunch. I thought it was a joke at first, but it wasn't."

"You sat with them?" I'm ashamed to say it, but my son sat at the cool table at lunch, and I was proud.

"Yeah."

"And?"

"We're friends. Stop. I shouldn't have told you."

Kyle had changed a lot. He didn't need glasses anymore. Strange. He had friends, but secretive ones. They spent a lot of time behind closed doors, whispering. He sensed when I stood outside to spy, opening the door with a new expression of disgust each time. But I thought, *maybe this is puberty for an only child with no dad.*

The suicides began the next day with the news of three parents who hung themselves. Two asphyxiated themselves in their garage. One parent left a note: "I miss Sadie. This person is not my child." I felt ill because I believed something was wrong with my son, as well.

The following week, a mother and father tried to kill their four children. The news footage of their arrest showed them screaming, "They are not our children. Something has happened."

Kyle walked in while I watched this, visibly startling me.

"Can I kiss you, Mommy?" He mimicked the way he spoke at six, pronouncing *kiss* as *kith*. He sensed my alarm and quickly added, "Just kidding. Those parents tried to hurt their kids. You wouldn't try to kill me, right, Mom?"

"Of course not. Why would you say or think such a thing?"

"You look at me funny. I am still Kyle."

"What do you mean, *still*?"

"I am Kyle, but I am something else, too."

I froze.

"We will make the world better— we—meaning all the children of the world. Anyone who stands in our way will need to go. Do you understand me, *Mom*?" He said

Mom, with a mocking tone and unnecessary forcefulness.

Staring into my son's face, I could see small octagons moving beneath his skin. "What happened, Kyle?"

"The blue rain. The octagons are inside Kyle. I mean me, and the other children. We're from another dying planet which is even worse off than this one, but we'll save this planet and live here. By the time we're adults, everything will be as it should be. You will need to play along and behave if you want to live, Mom. More blue rain is coming down all around the world."

SWEET TIME

By Joanna Michal Hoyt

Liberty paused inside the airlock door of the bunker where she'd spent the last nineteen years. She was as ready to face the world Outside as she'd ever be. She wore the tickproof suit, the respiratory mask, the gun, the knife. She'd triple-checked the contents of the heavy framed backpack. Sixty freeze-dried MREs. Water purification tablets. *The Complete Survivalist's Handbook*. Matches. Iodine. Bandages. Antibiotics. Painkillers. Cyanide pill.

Whatever else she needed she'd have to get from Outside, if the terrorists or the gangsters or the looters didn't get her first.

And if they did get her, that wouldn't be as bad as living in the bunker for another everlasting year with no contact with the outside world, hearing no voice but her own.

Liberty punched in her keycode. When the door slid back into the wall, she stepped Outside.

The light broke over her like a wave. Shutting her eyes, she heard: Wind rustling in leaves. Birdsong. (When had she forgotten to miss birdsong?) Mosquito whine. Snaps and rustles that could be assassins or raccoons. She opened her eyes, squinted.

Green all around her. Grass and low brambles close in. Trees surrounding the bramble clearing, more than half of them apparently alive.

She rose. Any attacker who'd seen her emerge would have grabbed her already. Any friendly observer would have come to help.

Maybe there wasn't anyone left Outside. Or Inside either. When the main newsfeed died, the rest of her survivalist pod had speculated that the official shelters had been hacked by bitter people who had failed their health and security checks. The pod wasn't worried, not then. They were still there in their private shelters. They'd inherit the earth. Then the pod's webfeed died. Liberty checked and rechecked her hardware, her software. She read novels aloud to herself to give the illusion of dialogue. Finally she left.

In the trees a wood thrush called, a liquid glide followed by a lilting laugh. Liberty laughed too, swallowed salt— sweat? tears?—and set off toward the thrush-song, stumbling on the hummocky ground, enjoying the ache of long-disused muscles. Her lungs ached too, demanding more oxygen than she could pull through the mask. Maybe the filter was clogged. She couldn't take it off. If any of the people who failed their screenings and couldn't afford private bunkers had survived Outside, they might be using chemical weapons, burning trash, breathing out superbugs…

But she needed air. She inhaled deeply, whipped the mask off. It was clogged with yellow powder—with pollen; she sneezed explosively and inadvertently gulped in unfiltered air, smelling wet greens, rot, roses, fruit.

She dropped the mask when she heard the scream. It was high, hoarse, barely human. Liberty crawled toward it. If she ever sounded like that, she'd want someone to come rescue her, or at least finish her off.

The sound was very close, and she couldn't see. She crouched beside a tree, slid the gun from its holster, rose, keeping her body pressed against the trunk, keeping her gun hand free...

"*Que haces? Son* nuestras *gallinas!*" The furious voice sounded close behind her. Liberty turned, gun first. Too late; Liberty knew that the shouter—who was obviously foreign and therefore dangerous—had the jump on her.

The child glaring at Liberty might have been eight or ten. Both her fists were braced on her hips. Her tight black braids stood out from her head. Her off-white dress was streaked with bluish-purple stains.

"What do you want?" Liberty demanded.

"Put that down, dummy! I'll tell Manruth!"

"Who else is here?" Liberty kept her gun aimed over the girl's head.

"Lancha?" Liberty didn't know what language that was, but the voice was deep and tense. When the young man—or boy, maybe—came crashing out of the woods, Liberty had the gun levelled at his chest. He froze, staring. The screaming resumed somewhere behind Liberty.

"Are you Manruth?" Liberty demanded. "What's happening back there?"

"He's Manuel, silly. Manruth's back home—" the girl began.

"Let Lancha go," Manuel said on a much higher note.

"Who's getting tortured?" Liberty demanded.

"You tick-sick?" Lancha asked.

"Lancha!" Manuel's voice had come back down. "Go! Tell Manruth there's a new one here and she's fear-sick. Go!"

"No," Liberty said. "You're not going anywhere, getting anyone, until you tell me what's going on here."

"Give me that, lady," Manuel, holding his hand out. "It's going to be okay. Put that down. You don't want to hurt anyone. You don't want to get hurt." He stepped cautiously toward Liberty. Liberty had seen that pose in old British flicks: unarmed officers, good people, advancing on criminals, saying *Give it to me...* Liberty holstered the gun, cursing herself for a fool.

"*Vete!*" Manuel said to Lancha, who ran off. "Come on," Manuel told Liberty.

"Manruth can help. But you've got to leave the gun behind."

Liberty froze as another scream tore the air behind her. Manuel reached for her. She couldn't let him disarm her. She couldn't shoot him. She ducked back around the tree and lunged downhill toward the screaming.

Something grabbed her foot. Something hit her head. Darkness swallowed her.

***

"She's coming round," a woman's voice said.

"Good!" said Lancha's voice.

Liberty sat up. Clutched at her head.

Felt at her hip: no gun. Felt at her side: she was lying on a bed, not a forest floor. Liberty opened her eyes gingerly. Lancha peered at her, and a short woman with a face very like Lancha's stood next to Lancha, fixing Liberty with a rather harder stare. Behind their heads was the underside of a thatched roof. Not very secure for a prison, Liberty thought. "What..." she began.

You'll be all right," the woman said. "I'm Luz, Lancha and Manuel's mother."

"What will you do with me?"

"Take you to see Manruth. If you can stand..."

Liberty stood, trying to act as if movement didn't hurt her head. Chin up, shoulders back.

Lancha giggled.

"Shoo, Lancha," Luz said. "Tell Manruth we're coming. Tell your brother—"

"I'm here," Manuel said, opening the door.

"You did the dangerous part," Luz said to him. "You can bring her in."

Liberty didn't like the sound of that. She realised unhappily that she was swaying.

"We can carry you," Manuel said.

"No! I can walk."

Manuel took Liberty's right arm, stuck the handle of a sunshade into her left hand, and escorted her outside.

Liberty squinted into the harsh light. There was a wall of dressed stone, twice

Liberty's height, a few yards to her left—to the south—with cages against it. Liberty forced herself to look at the prisoners.

The cages were full of rabbits. Between Liberty and the rabbits were rock piles and gigantic kale plants. To Liberty's right, similarly oversized eggplant and tomato bushes sprawled toward another high stone wall. Up ahead was a building with grapevines growing all over it. Misshapen black things, football-sized, moved between the plants in a horrible jerky way.

"What is this place?"

"A rain-year garden," Luz said behind her. "Go in and let Manruth have a look at you."

The door of the vine-wrapped house

creaked shut behind Liberty, cutting the painful light. She blinked at the circle of faces that watched her.

"This is her," Manuel said. "The one Lancha found near the mushroom clearing. Her name's Liberty, and she put her gun down when I said."

"I...I didn't mean to scare the girl," Liberty said. "I was afraid..."

"So I see," said a cello-toned voice. "You tick-sick, or just fear-sick?" The woman who had spoken had a weathered copper-coloured face and deep-set eyes. Her face and arms were skin stretched over bone, but her long broad-shouldered body was swollen as though with pregnancy.

"I don't think I can be tick-sick yet," Liberty said. "I haven't been out long enough."

"Out of where? The prisons opened years ago."

"I wasn't in prison! I had security clearance. I just thought I'd be safer on my own."

"You're a bunkie? You locked yourself in all these years?"

Liberty nodded.

"Are more of you coming?"

"I don't know. I was alone, and I couldn't talk to anyone in the other shelters."

"For how long?"

"I've been Inside nineteen years. Without communication, one year."

"*Ay Dios*!" Luz shook her head. "No wonder you're fear-sick."

"I'm not sick," Liberty insisted. "I didn't mean to scare your daughter."

"You didn't scare me," Lancha said, banging in through another door with a tin pail swinging from her hand. "Have some blackberries."

The smell took Liberty back to childhood summers in the overgrown pasture with her sister and Grandma Randall—both dead these twenty years—eating fruit sun-hot off the vine, scratching their hands and tangling their hair and laughing, laughing, laughing.

"You're not going to boil them first?" Liberty asked.

"They're better this way."

"You could die of germs."

"What you want to die of?" Lancha

asked.

"I don't want to die of anything," Liberty said.

"You got to," Lancha said.

Liberty swallowed hard.

"That's the truth," the cello voice said.

"I didn't hurt anyone," Liberty protested.

"Who says you did?"

"Then why is she saying I've got to die?"

"Cause you were born, *Dummkopf*," Lancha said.

"Lancha," said a man's voice, reproachfully. The speaker was a pale old man with a straw hat and a long grey beard.

"You listen to Levi," the cello voice said, "and don't go calling names."

Sorry, Manruth," Lancha said. "Sorry, Levi. Sorry, Liberty."

Manruth shifted her gaze back to Liberty. "But she gave you one of the true answers."

"I don't understand," Liberty said.

"Alles Fleisch ist grünes Gras…" Levi said.

"I don't understand…"

"All flesh is grass, and all the goodliness thereof is as the flower of the field," Manruth translated.

"What?"

The young man on her right sang—no, chanted; she couldn't make the words out.

"Ibrahim, I think she has only one language," Manruth said.

"'Ye were without life and He gave

you life; then will He cause you to die, and will again bring you to life; and again to Him will ye return,'" Ibrahim said. "It's better in Arabic."

Arabic! Liberty thought. If he spoke that, it was no wonder he hadn't come Inside; they wouldn't have given him security clearance.

"Men must endure their going hence, even as their coming hither; ripeness is all," said another woman's voice from the shadows.

"Edgar said that in *King Lear*," Liberty said, eager to show herself civilised. "When he was trying to save someone's life, not kill him!"

"No one intends to kill you," Manruth said. "Get that through your head."

"She said I had to die, and you agreed."

"We used to point that out in logic classes," said the woman who'd quoted *Lear*. "People didn't accuse us of attempted murder."

"But someone hit me over the head!"

"You ran and caught your feet in the berry bushes, and you fell and hit your head on a tree," Manuel explained.

"Oh," Liberty said in a small voice. "And you carried me where people could take care of me. Sorry."

He shrugged. "You were fear-sick."

"Have some berries," Lancha repeated. "Get some sweet while it lasts."

"The honeybees in our hives died again last winter," Manruth explained, "though we've still got wild bees to pollinate; a few sugar maples came back after the blight, but not enough so we can tap them yet. So now we're counting on fruit for sweetness, and the fruit-time's just begun, and who knows how long it'll last." She turned back to Lancha. "Pass them around."

"I have food in my pack," Liberty said. "I didn't come to take anything from you."

"What did you come for?" Manruth asked. "You had food. You seem healthy, except fear-sick. Seems you felt safe in your bunker, and you don't out here."

"I was alone. I was going crazy. Maybe had gone."

"You were safe dead," Manruth said. "And you wanted to be alive."

"You're going on about dying being okay."

"Dying, yes. Going into the Trees of Life. That's different from being safe dead."

Liberty, who was increasingly convinced that no one intended to kill her, inclined her head. "I'm glad you're so sure. Believing's a comfort, I hear."

"Maybe," Manruth said. "Some of us have that. My Levi does. I don't, but I've had my sweet time, and I'm going to the Trees of Life, and that's enough for me. You choose what's enough for you. Stay with us if you like, or go wherever else you like."

"We'd better talk about that," Luz said.

"We will, then," Manruth answered. "Seeing it was your kids..."

"I... I..." Liberty stammered.

"You explained, and you haven't got a gun now. Go look around, unless there's anything else folks want to ask you."

After a brief silence, Lancha handed Manruth the pail of berries. Manruth put her face down over the pail, inhaled deeply, then passed the pail on. Liberty raised her eyebrows.

"I can't eat now," Manruth said, gesturing toward her swollen stomach. Liberty felt her own stomach lurch. That thinness, that swollenness. Not pregnancy. Cancer.

"Someone take our visitor back outside. She looks like she needs fresh air."

"I'm not scared of her," Lancha said. "I'll go."

"I'll come too," Ibrahim said. Luz nodded.

"Who was screaming out there?" Liberty asked. "Why did you pretend they weren't?"

"Take her out, Lancha, show her," Luz said, laughing. *Laughing!*

Liberty took a sunshade, and followed Lancha and Ibrahim back out into the heat and light, groping for conversation. "They're nice eggplants," she said.

"Not bad this year. We just had two snows, and we lit fires so they didn't die," Lancha said.

"It doesn't snow in summer, and you can't grow eggplant in winter..."

"Lancha's young," Ibrahim said. "She doesn't remember months with no snow, or months with no ninety-degree days."

Liberty opened her mouth to answer, stopped. A misshapen black thing lurched toward her. White spots like mildew covered its deformed body. It lifted a small blunt-beaked head on a long narrow neck and gave the scream of a soul in torment. Then it pecked an orange grub off a potato vine.

"What is that?"

"Guinea," Lancha said. "S'posed to be guard animals, like geese but not so mean. Domingo said they'd scream to warn us about danger, and lay eggs too. But they scream all the time so we don't listen, and their eggs are tiny and they hide 'em. But they eat ticks so we don't get so much tick-sick, and potato bugs so we get better potatoes."

"All that screaming was *hens*?"

"Told you already," Lancha said, skipping ahead.

"You see," Ibrahim said, "there's not so much to fear." His left eyebrow arched up. "Maybe that's the best change that's happened since we thought the world was ending. What's left to be afraid of?"

"Plenty, I should think," Liberty said. "They said the prisons opened, so the criminals could be anywhere..."

"I am here. So are John, Lynn, Morgan, Ezekiel, Domingo, Concepcion, Raquel, Noor, and Jin. Domingo started us raising guineas. Noor and I designed the

Trombe wall. Some of the others who came out with us are in the Trees of Life."

"Come on," Lancha hollered. Liberty hurried after her; it was easier than apologising.

They splashed through the swamp containing remnants of the dry-year garden at the foot of the ridge—"Rained four inches last week, six the week before," Lancha said, "but there's good catfish here now"—out to an island crowded with curving canes of elderberry, the dark blue umbels bending the frail stems down almost far enough to touch the water. Liberty felt the slight resistance of the berries as they pulled free from their stems, the softness of overripe ones squashing between her fingers. Overhead willows swayed, making a shade and a sleepy music in the wind.

Lancha sang, less sleepily, in Spanish. "That's pretty," Liberty said. "What's it about?"

"The trees of life."

"I know one like that," Liberty said. "There grows a tree in Paradise, and the pilgrims call it the Tree of Life…"

"Levi says Paradise is what we had before we messed it," Lancha said, "but these are the Trees of Life."

"What?"

"Where they buried the folks from the first year."

"And you eat…"

"We eat the elderberries. The goats eat the willow."

"But you said people are buried here."

"Elders like rich soil. The new Trees-of-Life are pear, mostly, but we can't eat off those yet, they're too little."

"But…"

"Take and eat, this is my body," Lancha sang, popping a handful of elderberries into her mouth, holding another handful out for Liberty, who, much to her own surprise, took and ate.

***

Two weeks later, even Luz had accepted Liberty's presence. By then a cold snap had killed some of the tomatoes and eggplants (the ones nearest the Trombe wall and the rock piles had pulled through), raccoons had got into the corn (Liberty had helped shoot, and eat, some of them), and Liberty and Lancha had picked pail after pail of blackberries, so many that Manruth's people couldn't eat them all fresh. Liberty was boiling some down, Manruth lying nearby to breathe the blackberry smell, her husband Levi sitting over her and slicing tomatoes to dry.

"It's a good life," Liberty said, stirring carefully. "I see that now. I haven't been this happy since... I don't know when. But how long can it last? What would you do if a criminal came, or a lunatic? Someone armed and dangerous? Someone who threatened you or your children?"

She blinked in surprise to hear Manruth laughing. Then Levi joined, and then Ibrahim. When Liberty finally got the joke she laughed too, laughed so hard she wept into the pot, getting a little salt in with the sweet.

OBLITERATION

By Jodi Jensen

Abby stood on her tiptoes and craned her neck to see through the cluster of soldiers riding down the escalator. "Lance!" She jumped up and down, waving her arms the second she spotted his face.

His eyes met hers, and he grinned as he hoisted his bag higher on his shoulder.

She stepped back, out of the crowd of waiting families, and let him come to her.

It'd been a year since they'd seen each other, but he hadn't changed a bit.

Lance's face lit up as he emerged from the crowd. He dropped his bag and opened his arms.

She flung herself into the waiting embrace, burying her face in his shoulder as he lifted her off the ground in a bear hug.

"I missed you so much, Abbs," he croaked. His lips trailed kisses along her neck as he held tight to her trembling body.

"God, I missed you too!" The words had scarcely been uttered when the wail of a siren pierced the air.

As they broke apart, the waiting area filled with murmured voices as people glanced around. In the next instant, a loud blaring horn sounded over the loudspeaker.

Three long blasts, then a voice.

"All civilians, shelter in place. All military personnel, report to terminal 7B."

Abby's heart pounded as the message repeated three times. "What does that mean?" She didn't see anything but a steady stream of cars and sunshine through the window. Nothing unusual at all.

Suddenly, cell phones beeped, buzzed, and rang as the wireless emergency alerts went off. She whipped her phone out, but all the message said was to shelter in place. The ground shook beneath their feet and a collective gasp issued from the small crowd. "Lance?" She grabbed his arm, frantic. "The baby—I can't—"

"Come with me." He slid an arm around her shoulders.

They followed the rest of the soldiers out of the waiting area, but when they headed for the hallway of terminals, Lance hung back. "Where's Eric?"

"I left him with my mom." She swallowed the lump in her throat. "I have to go get him."

A shadow moved across the row of sliding glass doors where they stood, and the emergency horns blared again.

Lance yelled to be heard over the loudspeaker. "Go!" He pointed to the doors. "Get our boy. I'll call you the second I know anything."

Abby turned to run, but stopped and spun back around. "What if you can't? If I don't hear from you?"

"Wait for me at your mom's. And if

it's not safe there, you bring them to our spot. I'll find you, I promise." He pulled her in for a quick but fierce kiss. "Go, now!"

She dashed outside and high-tailed it to the parking garage, dodging people, vehicles, and abandoned luggage. The lights in the structure flickered, then went out. She grabbed her keys and hit the alarm button as she ran. In the near darkness, the flashing lights guided her to her Jeep.

A moment later, she emerged from the garage and slammed on her brakes as she stared at the sky. Black clouds stretched across the valley, and fireballs rained down, each one exploding upon impact.

She had only one thought. *Eric!*

With a glance at the clogged roadway

ahead, she gunned it, swerving onto the shoulder. Taking full advantage of her four-wheel-drive and careening past the horrified onlookers, she made it to her exit in record time.

Two right turns, and she pulled onto her childhood street.

Holy shit!

The whole block was in flames, torn apart by a fiery rock the size of a car.

She sped toward the first of the destroyed homes, her mom's red brick house, a scream stuck in her throat.

"Eric! NO—"

She lurched over the curb and onto the grass, parking as close as she dared, then jumped out. The front of the house was engulfed in flames, so she raced around to the back just as a basketball shattered a window and rolled across the lawn.

"Mom!" Abby yelled as her mother's head appeared in the opening.

"Thank God! I was trying to get us out of here!" Her mom disappeared, only to return a second later and thrust the crying toddler through the broken window. "Here, take him!"

"Eric!" Abby reached up and pulled her son into her arms. "Shh, baby, it's okay. Mama's here." She backed up a few steps, away from the smoke. "C'mon, Mom! Hurry!"

"I've got to get Lindy, I'll be right back."

Her mom vanished before Abby could object.

"Go bye-bye, Mama," Eric wailed against her shoulder.

"We will, baby, as soon as Gramma gets her kitty."

Just then, another fiery ball streaked across the sky, headed right for them.

She held Eric tight as she screamed for her mother.

But there was no time.

Abby ran for the Jeep, flung the door open, and scrambled inside with Eric still in her arms. She started the engine and laid on the horn. "Come on, Mom, we gotta go." Another few seconds and it'd be too late.

What the fuck am I supposed to do? Can't leave the baby in the car alone—can't stay here.

She snapped the seat belt around them both, and with a final glance at the house, and the fireball about to destroy it, she hit the gas.

The flaming boulder slammed into the house and exploded on impact, the force of it pushing the Jeep forward with its back-end off the ground.

They spun around, and by some miracle, didn't flip over as they crashed through the bushes, ending up a couple of streets over.

Abby sat there for a minute, sobbing and clutching Eric.

Her phone rang, startling her, and she fished around on the passenger seat for it.

Lance.

"Abby, where are you?"

"My mom…she…she's gone—"

"Eric?"

"I've got him." She kissed the top of their son's head. "He's safe. What's happening?"

"We're under attack."

"Attack?" She shook her head even though he couldn't see her. "From meteors?"

"Sort of." His voice softened. "Look, it's classified. Just get to our spot and I'll explain."

"Is it safe there?"

"Safer than where you are now. It looks like the populated areas are the heaviest hit. Now, go. I'll meet you there."

The phone went dead.

Abby glanced up at the sky, still black,

still raining down the fiery rocks, but none coming her way this second. She hopped out and quickly strapped Eric into his car seat in the back. "It's okay, baby boy, we're going to be okay."

Eric fussed, unhappy when she tried to get back in.

"Bun-bun," he cried, reaching over the side of his seat.

She leaned over and snatched up the stuffed bunny that must've fallen out of his diaper bag earlier. "Here you go, big guy, now let's go find Daddy."

With Eric settled, she got back in and headed out of the neighbourhood, once again grateful for her four-wheel-drive. The streets were a mess, crammed with traffic, pockets of fire, and people staggering around, dazed and injured.

She divided her attention between watching the skies and the roads as she made her way out of the city. Several times she'd had to change direction to avoid the meteors, and it was several hours before she made it to the mouth of the canyon.

Lance had been right, she realised, as she paused to look out over the valley before heading into the mountains. Engulfed in smoke and flames, the city had fallen.

Ahead, into the mountains, there were only a few rising columns of smoke.

She drove toward the campground they frequented during the summer months, praying it'd be safe. The further from the burning ruins of the city she got, the more the air cleared, and the better she felt.

"Almost there, baby," she said, talking more to herself than Eric.

A little while later, she pulled into the campground. As late as it was in the season, it was deserted, the ground covered in dead leaves and a brisk chill in the air.

She parked and got out to look around. It'd be dark soon, and there wasn't a soul in sight. Not a sound coming from anywhere. She went to the back of her Jeep for the emergency kit Lance always insisted she carry. She'd never had occasion to use it, but was glad now for his foresight.

She hadn't changed anything out in the year he'd been gone, so all the baby supplies were for an infant, rather than a toddler. Still, as she removed a too small diaper and a can of formula, she was beyond grateful that Eric would be taken care of.

After she got him changed and made a bottle, she got back in to wait for Lance. She had no cell signal here, no way to know how long he'd be, but she knew he'd come.

Hours went by before she saw lights approaching. Her heart thrummed heavily as she waited, half excited and half afraid.

No sooner had the strange vehicle caught sight of her than she heard him shouting her name.

She jumped out, grabbed the baby, and ran toward her husband. He barely had time to park the military Hummer and open the door before she was in his arms.

"Thank God," he said, his heartfelt exclamation muffled by her hair.

"What's happening?" Abby handed Eric over to him.

"There's a fleet of ships orbiting, they appeared out of nowhere and attacked by launching meteors at Earth." Lance put Eric in the backseat of the Hummer.

"Is it everywhere? Where do we go?"

"The military has underground bunkers, you'll be safe there. Watch the baby while I grab everything from the Jeep."

Abby reeled at the news, and it took her a second to realise what he'd said. "Wait, you're not staying there with us?"

"I can't, you know I can't, not until

this is over." He hurried to the Jeep and returned with the emergency kit. One more trip and he had the car seat. "Let's go."

As they were pulling out of the campground, the sky above lit up as a fireball streaked toward them.

"Hold on!" Lance swerved, but when the rock hit, a ball of flames exploded in front of them. The road crumbled as they skidded and spun around.

The Hummer's rear end fell into the edge of the crater left behind and the tires spun. He jerked the gear shifter and finally got traction. They bounced onto the road, heading back toward the city.

He grabbed her hand. "That was the road to the bunker."

Abby held tight to her husband. "Now

what?"

Never taking his eyes from the road, he kissed her hand. "Now we find another way.

Abby grabbed the handle above her window as Lance turned off the pavement at the first dirt road they came to.

"Shit," he muttered as he hit the brakes. "Look."

"I see it." Her hopes fell at the sight of the heavy, locked metal gate blocking their way.

"Screw it, I'm going." Lance backed up, floored the gas and rammed the gate, but it was stronger than it looked. He'd hardly made a dent. "Get in back with the baby."

Abby climbed over the seat and

buckled herself in next to the car seat. She kissed Eric's forehead, then met Lance's gaze in the rearview mirror. "Ready."

This time he backed up all the way to the pavement. "Hold on!" He slammed it into gear and gunned it. When they hit the gate, it bounced off the grill guard and flew into the air, landing behind them.

Pockets of fire burned among the trees, slowing their detour. Thick, clogging smoke filled the air, and Eric coughed.

"Down there." Abby leaned forward and pointed out the front passenger window.

Lance jerked the wheel and drove them into the bottom of a dry gully. The air was clearer, and the Hummer's headlights illuminated the rocky terrain at crazy angles as they lurched along. "I think we can get past the fire this way."

"How far is the bunker?"

"Top of the mountain, past the water towers."

Abby forced a smile at her son as he grabbed her hand and squealed at the bumpy ride. "What about the fire? Are we going to be safe if it reaches the bunker?"

Her husband nodded, the lines of his body, rigid. "It's deep underground."

After a couple of miles, the path veered away from the flames, and Lance drove the Hummer up the embankment.

Abby divided her attention between her son and the falling ash outside her window. Once Eric finally drifted off to sleep, she covered him with an old blanket from the emergency kit, then climbed into the front seat.

"It feels like we're the last people on the planet," she said, squeezing her husband's shoulder.

Lance gave a small smile. "We're not, I promise."

An hour later, they crested the mountaintop, and he pulled the Hummer into the trees and cut the engine.

Abby looked around, but didn't see anything except forest. "Where's the bunker?"

"Up ahead. I'm going to go have a look, make sure we can get in." He unbuckled his seat belt and grabbed a pistol out of the glove box. "Wait here. I'll be right back."

"But…what if—"

"Lock the doors behind me and move into the driver's seat. I'm leaving the keys, just in case."

Her stomach twisted in a knot, and she shivered. "In case of what?"

His hand cupped her cheek briefly. "In case you need to get out of here."

She wanted to protest, but with their son in the backseat, all she could do was nod and watch as her husband left. Once she'd scooted over and locked the doors, she sat gripping the steering wheel as she squinted into the darkness. It felt like hours with nothing to do but wait and worry, yet every time she checked the time, only minutes had passed.

Her heart skipped a beat when a figure

emerged from the shadows at last, and she reached for the ignition.

Lance…it was Lance…running for the Hummer.

She unlocked the door and slid over. "What's wrong?"

"The bunker's compromised!" He turned the key, and the motor roared to life. "Buckle up, we gotta go!"

Abby fastened her seat belt as Lance peeled out of the trees. "What the hell happened?"

"They've gone crazy in there, some kind of mind control by whoever's attacking us." Lance slammed on the brakes when a man appeared in the beam of headlights.

"Oh my God," she breathed.

The man, dressed in military fatigues, had blood dripping from a gash on the side of his head, soaking the whole right side of his camo jacket.

She glanced at her husband. "Should we help him?"

A movement outside caught her eye, and she turned back in time to see the man lift a bloody fireman's axe.

"Look out!" Abby screamed.

"Fuck—" Lance jerked the wheel as he floored the gas. But when he passed, the man swung the axe at the driver side window, smashing the glass. Lance ducked, barely managing to avoid having his head split open.

"Obliteration!" the man screeched.

In the back seat, Eric's high-pitched

cries joined the racket.

"Obliteraaaaation!" The man's repeated declaration faded as they sped away, leaving the bunker behind them.

"Jesus!" Lance's heartfelt exclamation was drowned out as he ground the gear shifter.

Abby scrambled into the backseat and tried to soothe the baby.

Eric's chubby little hands wound themselves around her neck and wouldn't let go.

"Shh, it's all right, big guy, Daddy's okay." She hummed softly and patted his head until he quieted. Her gaze went again to the rearview mirror, and she locked eyes with her husband. "Was that—"

"Mind control." He shook his head, his

face pale, even in the darkness. "It had to be."

"But why?" Abby blinked back tears. "Why would anyone do that?"

"A means to conquer," he said, from between clenched teeth.

"Now what?" Abby bit the inside of her lip. "What do we do?"

"I don't know. It makes sense they'd disable the military first, but damn, that'd been going on for hours from the looks of things inside. That means they attacked the bunker about the same time the meteors hit." Lance stared at the road, his voice softening. "How'd they even find—they've got to be picking up military frequencies? Oh—oh no—"

"What?" Her gaze darted to the front

windshield, but she didn't see anything outside. "What's wrong?"

"We need to ditch this thing. If they're picking up military frequencies, they'll be able to get a lock on the Hummer's GPS."

Beads of sweat sprang up on her forehead. The last thing she wanted was to be out in the open with the baby. "Can't you disable the signal?"

"I doubt it, I don't even know where it is. In fact, there's probably more than one, for backup." Lance slowed down and pulled into a dense grove of trees, then stopped. "Grab all of Eric's stuff, the blanket too. I'll get the rest."

Abby crammed her son's things in the diaper bag, her heart pounding the whole time, worrying the man with the axe might catch up to them. Once she had everything, she got Eric out of the car seat and cradled him in her lap while Lance finished packing.

"Ready?" He slammed the back of the Hummer shut and slung a duffel bag over one arm and semi-automatic rifle over the other.

She got out and slipped the diaper bag diagonally over her shoulder, then settled Eric on her hip. "Ready."

Lance clicked on a small flashlight. "Let's go."

***

Abby's arms ached. Her daily jogs had done nothing to prepare her for carrying a thirty-five-pound sleeping toddler all night over rough terrain. As dawn broke, she shifted her son yet again and stifled a yawn.

Lance stopped abruptly in front of her. "Look." He pointed down the slope at a half-dozen red rooftops peeking through the trees.

They watched for a moment, but didn't see any signs of life.

"Do you think it's safe?" Abby whispered.

Lance brought the rifle to his shoulder. "Only one way to find out. C'mon."

She trailed behind her husband, her anxiety growing as they got closer to the cabins. With every step, leaves crunched underfoot, making her cringe, but still nothing stirred.

Lance glanced back, then nodded at an older, blue pickup truck parked near the first cabin. He met her gaze and placed a finger over his lips.

Abby nodded and held a little tighter to Eric, grateful he was still sleeping. She fell back a few steps while Lance approached the truck. Once he'd looked in the windows and truck bed, he lowered the gun and motioned for her to come closer.

"Wait here while I check the cabin," he whispered.

Her gaze darted around the forested landscape, and she turned back to him. "I won't be able to see anything coming through the trees. I'd rather stay with you."

He hesitated, his eyes on his son, then agreed. "Stay behind me and keep quiet."

Abby followed him as he crept up the front steps and peeked in a window.

With a quick look over his shoulder, he shook his head, then lifted a fist to knock.

A soft *crunch* nearby had her reaching for her husband. She touched his arm, then motioned to the corner of the house. "Did you hear that?"

Lance turned and cocked his head as a loud rustling sounded in the bushes. He shoved the rifle tight against his shoulder. "Come on outta there!"

A brown snout appeared around the corner, sniffed, then suddenly a blood-covered Golden Retriever bounded in their direction, half barking, half whimpering.

Eric's head popped up as he let out a wail, and Abby stumbled backwards on the porch, away from the dog.

Lance held out a hand. "Hey there, it's okay, fella, I'm not going to hurt you."

The animal slowed, its tail swishing hesitantly.

"That's it," Lance cooed. "You're okay." The instant his fingers brushed the soft fur under its chin, the dog's entire body wagged in delight.

Abby breathed a sigh of relief. "Look, it's a doggie."

Eric clung to her neck, his small body trembling.

"It's okay. See Daddy petting him?" She took a step closer, trying not to cringe at the blood soaking its fur, and nudged her husband. "He's hurt."

"I don't think it's his." Lance ran his

hands over the dog. "I don't feel a wound anywhere. There's a collar, though." He fingered the tag. "Sadie. Is that your name, Sadie?"

The dog licked his hand, tail swinging with wild abandon now.

Lance shot Abby a quick look. "Wonder what happened?" He patted Sadie's head. "Where're your owners? Are they hurt?"

Eric finally peeked at the dog. "Oggie?"

"Yes, baby, that's a doggie." Abby frowned as she glanced around, even more uneasy than before. "Surely they wouldn't just leave her here like this."

Lance scrubbed a hand through his hair, pausing before turning to the front door once more. "Just let me look, I'll be quick, I promise. Whoever's blood that is might be inside."

"I don't feel safe out here alone." She was struggling to keep Eric in her arms. Now that he was fully awake, he was squirming to get down. "That person could just as easily be out here somewhere, or worse, the person who caused that," she said, with a nod at the blood-stained dog.

"I can check the inside faster than out here." He put his hand on the doorknob. "Sixty seconds. Stand with your back to the wall and stay alert." He snatched his pistol from his waistband and handed it to her. "Fire if you need me."

Biting her tongue, Abby backed up against the wall and nodded. "Hurry."

Lance twisted the knob, and finding it unlocked, slipped inside.

Abby settled Eric firmly on her hip, then looked at Sadie. "Can you sit?"

At the familiar command, Sadie sat, her tail sweeping the porch behind her in a continual show of happiness.

"Good girl," she muttered. "Now stay." Hopeful the dog would obey, Abby scanned the trees again as the seconds ticked by in her brain.

As promised, Lance was back before she'd mentally hit sixty, his face pale and drawn. "C'mon, we can't stay here." He jiggled a set of keys. "Let's see if that truck starts."

Abby's gaze flew to the door. "What did you see in there?"

"An old couple, both dead." He touched her shoulder. "Let's go."

She gripped her son a little tighter and followed Lance to the truck. "What about—" Before she could get the rest of the question out, Sadie ran down the steps and went straight to the truck, whining by the back tire.

"Guess she's coming too." Lance lowered the tailgate, and she jumped in.

Abby climbed in the front and snapped the seat belt around her and Eric both, relieved when the truck roared to life.

For the next half hour, Lance systematically checked five other cabins, all with the same result—no one was left alive—they'd all died violent deaths, their bodies ripped apart and shredded, he'd said.

At the end of the dirt road, back from the main cluster of homes, was one more cabin. A luxury two-story with floor to ceiling windows and a balcony over the front porch. Half of the roof was missing, and a thin pillar of smoke rose from behind.

Lance parked, and as with the other cabins, left her the pistol and went to investigate.

Eric fussed in her lap, so she set him in the middle of the bench seat. "Are you hungry, baby?" His little face lit up at that, and she smiled as she reached for the survival bag. "Let's see what we have in here." She rifled through the contents until she found a sleeve of crackers. "Here we go." While Eric munched happily, she kept watch for Lance. After several long minutes, he appeared from behind the cabin, his face grim.

She expected him to get back in the truck, but instead, he came and opened her door. "What is it?" she asked. "What'd you find?"

"There's one of them back there. It's dead." His mouth tightened in a deep frown. "I think it's what killed all these people."

"I want to see it." She moved to get out, but Lance stood in her way.

"I don't want you going back there alone, there could be more of them." He glanced at his son. "And I definitely don't want him to see."

"Then come with me," she said,

passing Eric over to him. "You can hang back a little, keep him turned away. I need to see it to know what we're dealing with."

Lance nodded, though his frown didn't diminish. "C'mon, Sadie, you can come too."

She followed her husband to the back of the truck as he let the dog out. "What if she runs off?"

"I don't think she will, not unless she's chasing something. She's used to people, and now hers are gone. We're all she's got." He patted his thigh as they headed around the side of the cabin. "Sadie, come."

With the dog trotting beside her and Lance right behind, Abby approached a pile of smoking metal.

Oh my God! It isn't a meteor, it's a ship!

Next to the smouldering remains lay a body. A human body. A man.

She turned to Lance, a question poised on the tip of her tongue.

"Over there." He nodded at the back deck.

As she approached, two more bodies came into view. One, a man with a gun lying next to his lifeless body. His throat and torso had been slashed to ribbons, and blood-splattered gore covered the otherwise pristine deck.

Her stomach turned.

The other body, the alien one, had a definite human-like form, with two arms and legs attached to a torso. What exposed skin there was looked like flat, grey clay. The head was bald, slightly larger, rounder, with only small holes where the ears should have been. Wide sightless eyes stared up at the sky, their solid black colour giving her a shiver. The hands were more like claws; long, skinny and ending with razor-like fingertips. Blood-covered, razor-like fingertips. The creature's mouth was small, no lips, just an opening filled with spiked teeth. The being wore a one-piece cargo-type of coverall with clawed feet showing at the bottom. The torso was riddled with bullet holes.

She covered her mouth and nose with one hand and held her stomach with the other as she turned back to Lance.

"Inside is clear." He passed her their

son, then grabbed hold of the dog's collar. "Take him inside, find whatever food and first-aid supplies you can while I burn this thing. Go around front, I unlocked the door for you."

Abby clutched her son to her chest and hurried to the front of the cabin, eager to escape the stench of blood and death.

Once inside, she glanced around at the ruined space, filled with a sadness she hadn't expected. It wasn't as if she knew these people, yet, somehow, she mourned the loss of the man who'd died defending himself and his home. And he'd taken the creature down with him.

"C'mon, kiddo, let's see what we can find." She set Eric down and took him by the hand into the kitchen, where she found the cupboard with pots and pans. She left it open for him to play with the contents while she rummaged through the other cupboards, setting canned goods, packages of dried fruits and nuts, and bottles of water on the countertop.

By the time Lance joined her, she'd also collected a can opener, a couple of knives, some plastic plates and silverware, and a small pile of bandages, hydrogen peroxide, and pain reliever pills.

"It's done," he announced. "Let's find something to put all this in."

"Can't we just load all of it in the back of the truck?"

"For now," he agreed. "But once the gas runs out, we'll be walking. We need to take what we can carry."

"I'll look around. I know the kinds of places I'd store backpacks and bags." She left her husband with Eric and went upstairs to search the bedrooms. She found what she was looking for in the hall closet and returned with two backpacks, a duffel bag, and a shoulder tote to which she'd added soap, towels, and sunscreen.

While she packed the supplies, Lance took one of the backpacks and used a knife to cut two holes in the bottom.

"What're you doing?" Abby frowned at him. "How're we going to carry anything in that now?"

"It's for Eric," he said. "Here, put this on and let me see what else I need to do to make this thing work." Obliging him, she stood still while he tightened all the straps, then picked up the baby and slid his legs through the holes. Eric giggled as Lance made a few more adjustments. "There we go, snug as a bug in a rug."

Abby walked across the room and back, testing the weight. "It feels pretty stable."

"We can take turns carrying him." Lance grabbed the other bags. "Let's get moving."

Once everything was loaded, they drove, sticking to the dirt roads, higher into the mountains, until the gas ran out. After that, they took as much as they could carry and walked.

At dusk, they came across an overgrown set of railroad tracks overlooking a valley.

Hand in hand, they trampled through the weeds as they followed the train tracks.

There had to be more survivors, they just had to find them.

ARRIVAL

By Kimberly Rei

When the sky sundered, opening the rift, no one cared. It had happened before.

When the lightning rained down in killing strokes, no one cared. They had seen it before.

When the connected world crushed portions of theirs and erased memories and friends, no one noticed. Why would they?

But the little girl climbing out of a taxi

scared them all. She looked around, imperious, as if she owned this world. Her voice slithered through the mind of every citizen, no matter age or caste.

"I have arrived. Kneel and tremble."

And when half the population dropped dead, they cared.

MUSE

By Liam Hogan

I am John's muse.

I am his divine inspiration, that sudden Eureka moment, the spiritual awakening on the road to Damascus, the unmistakable feeling of déjà vu. I am the blissful awareness of everyone else in the room, in the city, in the world. The feeling that everything is as it should be. I am rapture. I am enlightenment. I am Nirvana.

I am also his rage. His blinding headaches, his insomnia. I am the destructive, circular thoughts from which there is no escape. Thoughts that fester, that gnaw away at mind and soul. I am the seed of hysteria that rampages through the population, making people destroy the very fabric of their lives, making them hurt the ones they love. I am the madness that kills.

For this I am truly sorry. I have doomed a good man and the five he was sent to rescue. Their combined fates will deal a crushing blow to mankind's greatest adventure.

That my life, my ethereal being, will also end here seems trivial in comparison.

Before John, I would flit casually from mind to mind, soaking up a little knowledge here, letting it out there. Helping to make those unexpected and surprising connections that are so crucial to the advance of human understanding. I have journeyed between countless minds, joining with each in brief union, lightly touching their thoughts and their deeds and being nourished in return. Without me and my kind, you would still be banging rocks together.

In my youth I was hardly aware of my own existence, but with the slow accumulation of borrowed experience I have come to deduce what I am, what I do. There is still much that I do not know, that I will not now ever know.

I do not know how many of us we are, or how long we have been among you. I do not know how or if we breed. But I do know this: for all the benefits that I bring, I am a parasite.

John is asleep as I write these words. I write them with his left arm—it is easier to control than his dominant right—it does not have the same muscle memory to battle against.

Before he wakes, I'll take these scrawled notes and carefully hide them away. He suspects, I think. How could he not? But in the general craziness of it all, he has yet to put two and two together.

In the morning he will wonder why he is not as rested as he should be, why his hand is cramped, why his eyes are raw and tired, but by now he is getting used to these feelings and they are the least significant of his many worries.

It was hubris, of course. And chance; what were the odds to leap into a mind so focused, so precise, at the very moment his years of dedicated preparation finally came to fruition? If I were a younger being, I would not have been able to make a home here, I would have been rebuffed. Not all minds are equally open to me. But I forced my way in, wormed past John's stout defences, finding a narrow space within that steely trap.

That in itself should have been enough of an accomplishment and, having done so, I should have relaxed, basked in the fierce white glow of his single-minded purpose before allowing myself to be expelled, to take that unusual clarity of vision to some lesser mind, to briefly bestow a great gift upon it.

But how could I leave when I discovered what John was about to embark on? What an adventure! To travel beyond that thin envelope that is our mutual home. To ride mankind's biggest, most powerful engines, to share his most epic journey.

And so, having forced myself upon him, I compounded the error of my pride and forced myself to stay, binding to his rocky shore tighter and tighter, a clinch far more intimate than that of any lover.

I knew, of course, that I would not be able to travel all the way to Mars. I knew that. I am a parasite that fouls its own nest, that slowly poisons the mind it inhabits. My unions do not, cannot, *should not* last.

The longest I had ever spent in a single host before John was a mere week and that was the empty vessel of an imbecile, a dullard. Not like this, not like John's finely tuned, crystal sharp mind. He does not leave much room for an interloper such as I.

I sought only to experience the first steps: the exhilarating ride into the outer atmosphere, the weightlessness in those moments before the ion drive engages, a chance to see the whole of the Earth laid out before me.

I had not realised that from space there would be no other minds I could jump into.

I had not even known there was a limit to how far I could jump.

So now! Now I am stuck here, in John's mind. The precision tool it once was, it is no longer. Trapped and squeezed, I have spread thin and grown, like a cancer, with the same devastating results.

This is not the light touch that benefits us both. My tendrils span the entire width and breadth of his mind, and I know far too much about this rescue mission.

I know why Captain John Hamilton is alone in such a large craft and why the launch was not aborted despite the first telltale signs of my presence in his bio-readouts: his elevated blood pressure, his racing pulse, the jagged lines on his EEG.

Mars 1 departed Earth eight months ago, but the lander failed to detach from the orbiter. They cannot land and, with the lander still attached, nor can they return to Earth. So Mars 2, rushed to completion, is travelling fast and light, a crew of just one, with no lander and only just enough fuel to make it there.

Even so, the conjunction of planets is not as favourable as it was eight months ago; with every second that passes, Mars and Earth drift further apart.

The plan is, or was, simple: Mars 1 and 2 will rendezvous above the distant red planet and the crew and fuel and remaining supplies from the stricken craft will be transferred over. If all goes well they will return to Earth a year and a bit late, weak and malnourished but still miraculously alive.

It is not going to go well.

It will end in disaster, in the loss of both crews, and I am to blame.

Already Ground Control is wondering whether they can pilot the craft from Earth, if they can take it out of Captain John's increasingly erratic grasp. It is doubtful that they can dispense with him altogether. Without his nimble fingers and the ability to wield the tools designed for his limbs, his eyes, his mind, the complex systems will surely degrade, will surely fail.

Even the twelve minutes that the Mars bound signals will take, travelling at the speed of light from the radio transmitters of Earth, even this delay will be significant when the rendezvous is made. On this mission there is no margin for error.

I try to minimise my intrusions. While John is awake, I try to stay silent, to clear my mind, *his* mind, from the pressure that builds there. But still I feel the creeping insanity. The bursts of emotion, of rage. I have been here now for a little over three weeks and John's mind is as toxic to me as I am to him. It hurts. It *burns*.

Ground Control asks him to do constant tests, probing his mental agility, his memory, his dexterity. The results are not good and are getting worse. More worrying still are his brittle moods, his visible annoyance at each task, his confusion and fear when he finds what was once second nature is now beyond him.

Some of these reactions are mine, some of them are his. It is becoming increasingly difficult to tell the two apart.

Perhaps this is my ultimate fate: a loss of self, the union made permanent, two dissolved into a fractured, mutilated one. I am imprisoned in a tortured mind, looking out over the precipice towards the dark abyss of madness, sliding towards the edge.

I dream of lasting as long as I can. I dream of making it to Mars, of jumping to the mind of one of those five astronauts anxiously awaiting Captain John's arrival. Of sharing my time between them on the long journey home, eking out my existence until our triumphant return to a planet thronged with ready and willing hosts. What glorious relief I would feel!

It is fantasy. A sign of how far and how low I have fallen. By the time we reached Earth, I would have had to spend two whole months in each of the crew's minds. It cannot be done; the crew and I would be totally insane before we reached halfway. And I do not get to choose the minds I inhabit; I have never been able to do that. Each jump is blind. More than that, I have never returned to the same mind twice.

Do I inoculate them against my corrosive presence? Is each jump truly random or do I pick the most receptive host at any particular time? And what was it that for one fatal moment allowed John's diamond-bright mind to let me in, that attracted me to him? Was he the flame to my moth?

When John is not busy with the thousand and one checks and procedures he must perform each day, when he is not failing the tests that Ground Control sets him, when he is not being reminded to eat, to drink, to sleep, he has taken to staring in the mirror.

What does he see there? Does he see me? Is he wondering who or what he is becoming, or trying to contact the man he once was?

It is disconcerting and I feel impatience, annoyance, a desire to break the contact, to wrest complete control of his body from him, force him away from his unnerving study.

His wordless contemplations highlight the stark physical effects I am having on that most sensitive of canvases. His face is thin and pinched. His eyes are watery and reddened, dark hollows form beneath them. His lips are cracked and bleed constantly, and his tongue is a dull, furred off-white.

He looks tired. He looks ill. He looks *crazed.*

If he could see me staring through those same bloodshot eyes, what would he say? Would it be a surprise to me? Or would I hear my own thoughts, my own words?

Would he ask who I write these pages for?

Who is it that I expect to read this rambling apology? What good can it possibly do? Do I really think anyone will believe these scrawled words, or will they merely attribute them to an isolated man's crumbling sanity?

I do not know the answers. Perhaps I write for no one. Perhaps my voice is already lost, and this is a mere distraction.

I know only that while I write, while I take control of his hand and coerce it into the infuriatingly precise movements that these letters require, I am calm. I do not feel the need to rant and rave. The blackness recedes and I take a half-step back from the edge of the abyss.

If this mission fails, as surely it must, will man ever travel this way again? Or will he remain bound to his fragile planet, growing in number, poisoning himself and all on it, just as I poison John's mind?

There is one thing I can do. One last, desperate measure that I can try. It might not work. It might not be enough to save John, to save this risky mission.

I could relinquish my stranglehold on his mind. I could leap, rending us asunder.

But here in the inky vastness I will not find another host, will not slip into a receptive mind with its own unique set of experiences, of thoughts.

I would be casting myself into nothingness. Into space. Into oblivion.

A noble sacrifice, perhaps. Is this why I write? A suicide note?

If it were done, 'tis best done quickly. Before fear makes a child of me once more.

So look for me when you gaze upon the heavens, the heavens you will one day make your home. Look for me and wonder.

I was John's muse.

First published by Blyant Publishing, 2016

A BLUE DOT, A WHITE DOT

By Michael Anthony Dioguardi

I can't see! I can't fucking see!

No! Don't crumble, stop! Christ, my tether is threadbare. I have to dig my feet in. I can't get my hand out of this biner. Oh shit! More wind! Armstrong! Armstrong! No! he's gone.

I don't want to die! My tripod is still holding, for now. Mic's still broken—just fuzz and static.

I can see a bit ahead. Stanton, she's still fighting with her cable. She's flat on the ground. Is she—she's readjusting her cable, oh dear God! I can see another cyclone spiralling up towards us. No! Her body trampolines above my head into the ether. My visor is so full of rusted soot— I've lost sight of her already. It's starting to crack.

It's me and Mooney up here. Mooney's behind me; he's off his feet. He's struggling to regrip his tether. His tripod is unearthing. He's the size of an ant now, shrinking down the infinite vastness of the mountain.

There's nothing in front of me except for the rushing of brown particles. A trillion needles sink into my suit. I swear I can taste the foreign soil through my visor. My intestines are flooding my legs with their anxiety-filled acid. My head's throbbing. My jaw is chattering against my tongue. I can feel the wrinkles on my face perspire.

This is it. This is how our mission will end.

I wonder what they will say about us? I wonder how my family will feel? Our bodies will likely not be found for years. Not until the next expedition, if that ever happens.

They said it would be easy. It would be a straight walk up. At the top, you wouldn't even realise you were on an incline. That's how big it is—the tallest mountain in the solar system. What a load of shit.

I feel another gust coming. I can see the swirl in the crater behind me. The lightning pierces through the rusted smoke and illuminates the horizon. There's an aperture in the clouds.

Such a marvellous sight.

My feet are completely buried. I guess this is how Opportunity felt all those years back. Dust ran through his robotic veins and seized his mechanical heart.

My tether's about had it. The crack in my visor is growing. The canal of tears running down my cheeks twinkles in its reflection.

The sky is stunning.

I can't hold much longer.

There's a blue dot out there on the

horizon. It's not alone. There's a white dot behind it—so bright, so beautiful.

I can't—

First published by 365tomorrows.com, 2020

NORTH OF 25

By Mike Adamson

When I was a kid, my family lived on a small farm just south of Intercity 25 that cut across the dry land outside Shellton City, on the warm southern continent of Gagarin's World. Outside the jungle belt, the land was good to farm, and we grew dryland crops. We did okay.

The number *25* has had meaning for me my whole life through, not that I've ever understood its cosmic significance, or if there *is* one. It's just there, following me all my days. My dad used to tell me not to go north of 25; that was no-man's-land, and crossing the highway was dangerous. A long blacktop as far as the eye could see both ways, commuters went through faster than short legs could get from one side to the other. One time I crossed over, wandered in the reaped fields over that side, and it was like forbidden fruit, and oddly enough the price was twenty-five licks. I didn't do it again for a long time.

We had twenty-five vehicles out in the sheds and an overdraft with Colonial Credit PLC that never seemed to dip below twenty-five grand. My alarm was on for 5.25 every morning. By fourteen, I was a damn good reaper driver and could bring in the einkorn from the back paddock in just under twenty-five minutes—every year, the same figure. I wondered where I would be when I was twenty-five years old.

Things started to go bad on Gagarin's when I was a kid. This was before the war, when the wrong sort of government got in. Other colonies out there started looking down their noses at us, like we were the skanky sister of the Great Human Adventure. Maybe they were right. But the capital, New London, was as grand a city as you'd ever want to see, the shipyards were booming on military contracts even before the Sendaaki attack—something many found highly suspicious, as if those responsible for the human military build-up kinda knew something the rest of us didn't. But at street level it was a home, like any other, and we accepted surveillance as the price of stability.

All this was happening back in the twenty-fifth century, of course, those troubled last decades. You just lived through them; they rolled off you as normality. By the time I was an older teen, I had self-image to think about, spent 2500 creds on a bush-beater aircar as old as my dad and got into trouble all over the region. Never made it to twenty-five brushes with the law, but they did take that many points off my licence. I hit the gym, of course, as one does. I remember my instructor giving me cardio on the stationaries and telling me to just keep the speedo north of twenty-five for an hour as a good place to start.

The number has never quit all my days through. My first apartment was in the block at 25 Lakeshore Drive—a cheap slum with a grand name, for workers at the shipyards where I had my first apprenticeship as a drone controller. I couldn't help noticing I had twenty-five mech-units on my roster. I was good at it, and between working out and running construction droids, I was gaining an identity.

When the war came they announced the formation of a Marine division on Gagarin's. And, being young and stupid, I put my hand up. The hardest thing I ever did; I wished a thousand times—not twenty-five—that I'd had more sense, but I got the hang of it eventually. The unit was arbitrarily allotted the number…you guessed it, 25th Marine Division. There I was, Private Joel Haddon, with the gold '25' on my shoulder, wearing it like the ironic brand of my life. I was away a long time; I saw action in the festering battles of the Acrasius Sector. I was in the jungles of B-6 for a while. In fact, I did two tours, which, including transit time, was a total of twenty-five months active.

I got email and vids from home; of course, everyone did, but the censors were pretty strict. I knew something was wrong on the farm; Dad had been drafted into industrial service; Mom and the girls were running the place and hoping agriculture didn't lose its limited status of 'protected occupation' before the end of things. Money was tough, and the government was not helping, which meant all sorts of greasy middle men came out from under rocks with offers of loans. A quick twenty-five grand looked attractive. I told them to resist the impulse as long as they could, but I knew a day would come when they had to take out a loan to cover debts. I couldn't send home enough to make a difference, and when the war was done, my regiment demobilised twenty-five lightyears away, a cost-saving measure on the part of the aligned governments of the Middle Stars. It took me months to get back. I worked any job I could find to raise the price of an economy liner ticket; I held onto the military gratuity, never spent a red cent—

the family needed it—but by then we'd lost touch.

I got back on my twenty-fifth birthday. The farm was sold, some national combine had it, and the family was in a work shanty outside the capital. Of course, with the end of hostilities, all Fleet contracts were cancelled, ships were going into storage at a high-orbital parking zone to await the next call to arms, and floods of ex-servicemen and women were straggling home, looking for work. The economy was in shreds, and the black market was booming. Twice I was offered jobs as an arm-twister for the wrong sort, and actually considered taking them—until I discovered the identity of the loan shark who ran my family out of our home and handed it to the big guys. Then I was only interested in payback. I had a word with other veterans, did some favours I'm not proud of, picked up intel and a decent weapon, and one night paid a visit. How many rounds did I use settling the account? Bet your last credit, it was north of twenty-five.

I might do as many years if they ever catch me, but there are careers to be found out there for those with the skills, and I'm working a passage to the frontier where new colonies are coming. It's the twenty-sixth century now, and the date no longer mocks me. I don't know what I'll find, but I'll bring my family out here if I can win my fortune.

Twenty-five million would be nice; with rejuvenative biotech, I have centuries in which to work, scheme and try, but supposing I live to be a thousand, I'll never forget that farm I called home, far away on Gagarin's, by the blacktop they called Route 25.

First published in *Uprising Review Magazine*, 2017

DREAMSCAPE

By R.A. Goli

Reina's skin prickled as she watched the curtains flutter unnaturally. Her cat slept on the couch, seemingly oblivious to the fact the material was moving in circular motions, despite no doors or windows being open. Her pulse spiked when her virtual assistant blasted classical music without her voice command. The startled cat ran from the room.

Don't panic, could be a glitch.

A figure appeared from the end of the hall. Pale and saturated, the wet woman raised her head and smiled maniacally at Reina. The staccato of her heart quickened. She knew what she was seeing. The bottom of the woman's skirt floated a foot above the carpet, yet Reina couldn't see her feet.

"Get the fuck out of my house!" she screamed, trying to sound brave, but the high-pitch of her voice betrayed her fear. Thoughts ran through her head in an instant. *I just bought this place. Will I have to move?* The spectre rushed forward, and Reina bolted through the closest bedroom door.

And entered a theatre. The room was dimly lit, and virtually empty; barely thirty seats were occupied. The stage was surrounded by deep brown curtains; there were no props. Reina understood it was a rehearsal performance. It must have been an amateur production, for she was playing one of the leads. In front of her was a boy from her high school class, Jake—now a man—and he was leaning forward and kissing her. They weren't great friends in high school, in fact, he had once called her 'Thunder Thighs', but she was a grown woman now, and those things no longer mattered. She wondered if her husband would be upset at her kissing someone else. Surely, he'd understand. A burst of woos and clapping followed, and she scanned the audience of her fellow cast members, all smiling and appreciative. After rehearsal, they decided to go for coffee. When she stepped outside, she was alone.

Reina marvelled at the vividness of her surroundings. Tree trunks and branches were pure white, with bright purple leaves, the grass beneath her feet was dark blue. Clouds rolled lazily across a green-hued sun, then opened up and rained shimmering water droplets on her. They were warm and sparkled like glitter. Reina laughed.

A small part of her now understood she was dreaming. The interface on her watch was flashing; pulsating crimson like the beating of her heart. While it did monitor her heart rate, blood pressure and numerous other health-related activities, the blinking red light was indicative of a major malfunction of the Dreamscape app.

Unfortunately for Reina, she had neither a husband nor a cat, so there was no-one to wake her. Eventually a colleague might notice her absence from work, but by then it would be too late.

She would be stuck there forever.

DIGITAL DREAMS

By Raven Corinn Carluk

"Thank you for coming, Mrs. Strauss. I'm Dr. Fisher, the new head of programming on your husband's case." The young doctor gestured at a chair before taking his own beside Dr. Armstrong.

Diane Strauss took her seat, assessing the programmer. He was a neuroscientist, same as Dr. Armstrong and her husband, but half their age. She'd learned the earmarks of a man fresh out of residency, and Dr. Fisher bore them all. "You have news of my husband?"

Armstrong lowered his eyes, taking a sip of bourbon. He'd worked with her husband for twenty years and was as deeply invested in his return as she was, but he was also a realist. The odds of waking from a coma worsened by the day—even digitally induced ones.

Fisher, however, was young and hopeful, still eager to work in the field of Holographic Projection Constructs with the ground-breaking Drs. Strauss and Armstrong. "Not news, per se, but a radical new treatment. I've had great success on normal patients, and I'm confident this will work on Dr. Strauss."

Diane sighed, exasperated and weary, then pulled her cigarette case from her purse. Fisher tried to tell her not to light up, but Armstrong waved the younger man off. She took several angry drags before she met Fisher's gaze. "All right, tell me about this brand new treatment that will finally bring my husband out of that world of his." Diane almost asked for a drink, but she didn't intend to stay that long.

Fisher's shoulders drooped, his eyes lost a little of their gleam. She'd taken some of the wind out of his sails, but not enough to prevent him from discussing his proposal. He coughed once, waved non-existent smoke from his face, and began speaking.

"Dr. Strauss's work is revolutionary.

Truly groundbreaking. During my residency, I worked with his base model and accident victims in comas. There was much evidence that simply being in the Construct was good for their health. Our ward had higher recovery rates than ones without."

She pointed her cigarette at him, then flicked ashes onto the floor. "I know all about my husband's work." Diane narrowed her eyes as she took another drag. Abraham smothered a cough that she suspected was a laugh.

Fisher swallowed hard, glancing at his fellow doctor. "Yes, well, I was the first to try something markedly different. I changed the program, and the success rate jumped to almost ninety percent." He paused, swallowed again, and dared to meet her eyes. "I believe we might be able to reach Dr. Strauss."

Diane shook her head once, finishing her cigarette. "And what are you doing that no one else has figured out?" After six years, she wasn't one to get her hopes up, but she would at least hear the young man out before authorising his attempt. Nothing reached her husband inside his digital dreamscape, but she always let them try.

"I change the parameters of the Construct. Keep making little changes until the mind realises that the Projection isn't reality and wants to find a way to wake up." Fisher's voice grew in volume until it rang with pride.

Diane arched a brow, glancing to

Armstrong. He nodded, tipping his glass to her. "What kind of changes?" She leaned forward, planting an elbow on the arm of the chair.

Fisher grinned as if she'd already said yes. "Small historical facts, like celebrity deaths. Then popular movie quotes. If the subject doesn't respond to that, the changes get increasingly more ludicrous. Outright lies on the news. The least qualified man elected president. Tradition rejected for a hundred genders and sexual identities. Flat earth. Chemtrails. Globalist corporations genetically modifying food into poison.

"With your help, we can come up with a tailored experience. Whatever you think would make Dr. Strauss take a second look, make him question his reality." Fisher had moved to the edge of his seat, gesticulating wildly as his excitement increased.

Diane tapped a manicured nail against her chin, thoughts churning in her head. Fisher's plan certainly had the beauty of having never been tried. She refused to feel hope, but she also wouldn't let an opportunity to save her husband slip by. Neil wouldn't give up on her, would certainly create edgy, new techniques to bring her back.

"He's always loved Luke Skywalker," she said after a pregnant pause. "Maybe if he died in a new movie?"

Fisher paused, stared at her. "It's just crazy enough to work."

DEATH IN THE RAIN

By Stephen Herczeg

Tantarus was a shithole of a planet. It was cold. An almost continuous rain of water mixed with a heavily diluted cocktail of calcium hydroxide and sodium peroxide, which stung unprotected skin and eyes. But Tantarus was a jump station nestled halfway between Earth and the outer reaches.

As humans spread throughout the

galaxy, Tantarus had taken on a life itself, becoming both a transport hub and a lair for criminals and smugglers. Law enforcement didn't care how Tantarus was run or who occupied it, as long as the traffic was allowed to run freely, they left it to itself.

It was the prospect of tracking down the scum of the galaxy that had brought Locke to such a godforsaken place. His business was hunting bounties. He filled the void left by the regular cops, operating just inside, and sometimes outside, the law.

Word had come across the sat-net that Dallas Brand had arrived on Tantarus. Brand was the leader of a rim-world resistance group, but the scuttlebutt within the hunter community was he just liked killing people. A bounty of ten million credits had been raised on him. Locke was the only hunter on Tantarus at that point in time. Lucky for him. Unlucky for Brand.

It had taken several days of trawling the local bars and dives to gather enough info about Brand's whereabouts, but now Locke was confident he had him. Soon, he'd be on the move. One helpful informant—that Locke had left in a puddle of his own blood and teeth—told him through his newly aerated mouth that Brand was headed to Earth to begin a new revolution against the Terran Government. His transport left in two hours.

Locke peered across the street through the teeming rain. There was movement in the apartment building. Two figures crossed in front of the windows, throwing a shadow puppet show across the translucent blinds.

Locke was sure the bigger shadow was Brand. He was rumoured to be two metres high and about a hundred and fifty kilograms.

A small bright crack appeared at the doorway. This was it. Locke had to move now. His hand dropped to his hip and folded around his pistol. As he stepped forward, he felt cold metal press against the nape of his neck, naked beneath his hat. He stopped dead in his tracks.

"Fuck," he whispered under his breath.

"Now, why would a bounty 'unter be swannin' around in the rain, I wonder?" said a deep voice cutting through the drizzle.

Locke turned and stared into the single eye of death pointed at his forehead. His eyes darted up and took in the full height of Brand. The rumours were wrong. He was almost three metres high. A detail that mattered little right now.

Brand smiled down at the bounty hunter.

"I am gettin' very sick of you scumbags followin' me everywhere, and I've only got one fing to say to you."

"What?" asked Locke.

"You're toast."

Brand squeezed the trigger.

COSMIC IGNITION

By Zoey Xolton

Starfleet Captain Rosa Drakemoore, call-sign 'Cinders', guided the *Red Aster* through the wormhole. Stars, planets, and galaxies blurred together in an eye-bleeding kaleidoscope of blazing colour.

The hull shuddered as they breached terminal velocity.

"Cinders!" came the cry over comms. "We have a breach! I repeat—"

Milliseconds later, before Captain 'Cinders' had time to jettison the ship's secondary thrusters and loading bay, a great metallic scream ripped through the *Red Aster*…the hull's breach peeling open like a sardine tin.

Oxygen, rocket fuel, and friction became one. The pride of the fleet ignited, combusting instantaneously…littering the wormhole with smouldering cinders.

ABOUT THE PUBLISHER

BLACK HARE PRESS is a small, independent publisher based in Melbourne, Australia.

Founded in 2018, our aim has always been to champion emerging authors from all around the globe and offer opportunities for them to participate in speculative fiction and horror short story anthologies.

Connect

Website: *www.blackharepress.com*

Twitter: *@BlackHarePress*

BLACK HARE PRESS

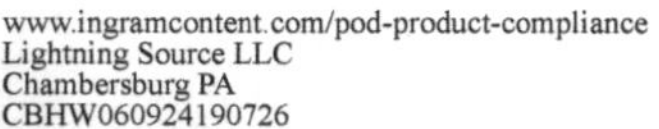

www.ingramcontent.com/pod-product-compliance
Lightning Source LLC
Chambersburg PA
CBHW060924190726
48286CB00002B/632